KEEPERS OF THE VAULT

FIRE AND GLASS

Published by Clockwise Press Inc., 201 Taylor Mills Drive
North, Richmond Hill, Ontario, L4C 2T5

www.clockwisepress.com

christie@clockwisepress.com   solange@clockwisepress.com

10 9 8 7 6 5 4 3 2 1

Library and Archives Canada Cataloguing in Publication
Chan, Marty, author
Fire and glass / Marty Chan.
(Keepers of the vault) Issued in print and electronic formats.
ISBN 978-0-9939351-5-2 (paperback).'
Title.
PS8555.H39244F57 2015   jC813'.54   C2015-905929-1
C2015-905930-5

Cover Art by Harlee Noble
Lantern image via Wikimedia Commons
Cover and Interior design by CommTech Unlimited
The text of this book is set in Open Dyslexia font.
Printed in Canada by Webcom

MIX
Paper from
responsible sources
FSC
www.fsc.org   FSC® C004071

Keepers of the Vault

Fire and Glass

Marty Chan

CLOCKWISE
PRESS

Many hands make light work.
For their helping hands, I'd like to thank
Christie Harkin, Solange Messier,
Wei Wong, and Michelle Chan.

M.C.

1 : INVISIBLE GIRL

Nothing said lonely more than being the new kid at school. The feral cats that were my classmates scurried off to their hideaways, abandoning me with the other runts. I don't know where they went, but I knew if I tried to follow them or get their attention, they'd flash me an indifferent look and run away.

I'd hoped today would be different. Maybe I could actually make eye contact with one of them so I could confirm I wasn't just some ghost wandering the dusty tomb that was MacKenzie King School.

Nothing made me feel more invisible than the ancient hallway. Built before my grandparents were born, the school showed every one of its years. The rusted pipes above the hallway dripped on the cracked floor tiles. Water stains marked the faded paint on the walls and the floor bubbled from flood damage. The corridor reeked of stale B.O., mould, and body spray. The kids ignored the rundown place with the same indifference they ignored me.

At my old school, I had grown comfortable with my rank in the social order. I was somewhere near the top, thanks to my best friend Jen and her ability to snark out pretty well anyone. She had a reputation for cutting down others, but she only picked on the people who pretended to be better than everyone else. She never preyed on obvious targets or the ones who couldn't return fire. Everyone adored her because of this, and as long as I was with her, the kids liked me as well. I could use Jen right about now to snark out the self-important kids strutting toward the cafeteria, led by a Goth girl in Doc Marten boots and faux leather.

Mom had moved us from our quiet suburban home on the outskirts of Edmonton to the inner city to be nearer to her downtown office job. After Dad decided he'd had enough of Mom and me and took off on us, we needed to save money. That meant I had to start over in the middle of my grade nine year at MacKenzie King. Unlike my father, I hated starting over. Different teachers, different students, different everything. I wanted my old life back with my old room, my old hangouts, and my old friends.

I found a clean spot at one of the grungy

tables and opened my paper bag lunch. A bottle of orange juice crushed a stale sprout and cucumber sandwich at the bag's bottom. I rescued my sandwich, unsealed the plastic bag, and peeled my lunch out. The cucumbers slipped out of the bread like the paper debris of a kindergartener's failed art project. I stuffed the soggy white and green discs back between the slices. I missed the fried rice and barbecue pork buns my grandmother used to make for me. Now I was stuck with whatever Mom could pull together before she headed off to work.

I scanned the room as I bit into the sandwich.

A boy sat at a nearby table. His bangs hung over his brown eyes. You could tell a lot about a person by the way he carried himself, and this guy was trouble. He propped one foot on the empty chair beside him, showing off his crud-encrusted blue jeans. No one else sat with him, but his casual slouch suggested he couldn't care less about the company he kept.

He rubbed his finger across the side of his mouth as he grinned at me. I scrunched my face, unsure of the signal. His tongue darted out and licked the corner of his lips.

Ew, I thought. *Was he coming on to me?*

He licked again. I stared at my sandwich and pretended to ignore him.

Moments later, the squeak of rubber-soled footsteps stopped beside me.

Please don't be him. Please don't be him. I slowly peeked up at a Bowser T-shirt hanging loosely over a scrawny frame.

"You have a sprout hanging off your lip."

My hand instinctively reached up to my lips. He was right. My face reddened as I plucked the sprig out of my mouth and laid it on the plastic wrap. He wasn't trying to come on to me.

"Name's Dylan Parker," he said. "Saw you in science class yesterday. You're new here."

I nodded.

"What's your name, sprout girl?"

"Kristina Mah," I said. A couple of half-chewed bits of sandwich tumbled out.

Dylan smiled. "First time with your new mouth?"

I covered my mouth and tried to swallow.

"Don't worry about it, Kristina. Everyone's staring at their smartphones. The only way you could get them to look up is if you yelled." He glanced at the crowd and shouted, "Zombie!"

Several kids stirred. One rolled her eyes at Dylan and resumed texting. No one cared. A hint of a smile crept across my face. "I see you're not obsessed with tweets and pics."

He shrugged. "Can't play decent games on

a smartphone. If someone could come up with a *Mega Man* app, maybe I'd play. *Mega Man* is an old Capcom game," he added.

"Dr. Wily always creeped me out," I said.

He raised an eyebrow and nodded. "I'm impressed. You an old-school gamer?"

"Does Mario have an evil twin?" I said. "You want to split the rest of my sandwich?"

He laughed. "No, I'm not a fan of cucumber farts."

"What's your favourite game?"

"Ever hear of *Hogan's Alley?*"

"Nintendo? I loved that one," I said. "The gun was glitchy, but the game was still fun. I always shot the old man."

"You know you're not supposed to shoot bystanders, right?"

"Oh, really? I wish I knew that before."

He grinned. "I played *Grand Theft Auto* before it was cool."

Though I figured my nerd status was growing with each minute I talked games with Dylan, I didn't mind the company. The bell interrupted our conversation.

"What class do you have?" he asked.

"Language arts," I said.

"Oh right. You joined a couple days ago. Follow me. I know a shortcut."

He led me into the mosh pit of students in the school hallway, pushing past the slackers leaning against the walls and around the jocks, who refused to get out of the way for anyone.

"Coming through. Radioactive isotopes. Move aside. Dangerous materials." Dylan rattled off odd-ball warnings as we navigated through the crowd.

"What are you doing?"

He glanced back. "It's a game I play to see what gets people's attention. So far, not much. Once, I thought a girl noticed me when I said I spotted Taylor Swift but it turned out she was just talking to her friend."

"You're the invisible man," I joked.

"Yeah, unseen to everyone except my own kind."

My heart sank with the realization that Dylan was right. Not a single person even glanced my way. We climbed the steps to the second floor. As we reached the landing, Dylan made the sign of the cross.

"Are you religious?" I asked.

"Only in this stairwell."

"What do you mean?"

"Just walk fast."

He sprinted up the stairs, two at a time, and then waited for me at the top as I hauled myself up by the banister.

"Want to fill me in there, Mega Man?" I asked, panting.

"Just a superstition," he muttered.

We continued in awkward silence to the language arts classroom. Dylan split away and headed to his desk while I headed for my seat at the back.

I'd just pulled out my books when the Goth girl with the Doc Marten boots stopped in front of me. "You're. In. My. Chair."

Seriously?

"Sorry," I mumbled as I got up and scanned the room for another empty seat.

Our teacher shuffled in, sporting a tweed jacket with elbow patches, a green bow-tie and black slacks covered with cat hair.

"Social time is over," he announced. "Take your seats."

The cool kids reluctantly broke off their conversations and eased into their desks.

"Today we move on to monsters. In particular, Frankenstein's monster."

Mr. Carlton tapped his computer keyboard several times. At the front of the room, the SmartBoard flickered on. A dim black-and-white image of a square-headed man appeared on the screen. The metal bolts sticking out of his neck gave away his identity—Frankenstein's monster. Then another image phased in over the monster—an old-fashioned lantern with a candle burning within.

I glanced around the class wondering if anyone else saw the same image. Mr. Carlton had his back to the SmartBoard. The other students slouched in their seats, barely paying attention to the image.

Slowly, I raised my hand. "Uh, sir. I think something's wrong with the projection."

Mr. Carlton squinted up from the keyboard. The image of the lantern was gone. Now only Frankenstein's monster stared at the classroom. He sighed. "This is a publicity still from a time when movies were black and white. Shocking, I know, but now you can tell your friends you saw something before HD was invented. So, let's examine what Frankenstein's monster represented."

Our teacher scooped up a black marker and strolled to the whiteboard. He began to scrawl the words "Dangerous Knowledge."

Beside him, the SmartBoard screen flickered again and the lantern returned. No one else seemed to notice. They just scribbled notes in their books.

Across the room, I saw Dylan stiffen.

A girl's voice whispered, "Help me."

The only other person in the room that seemed to have heard the voice was Dylan, who clapped his hands over his ears. On the screen, one of the lantern's glass panels began opening by itself and the flicker of a flame ignited on the wick. I could just make out eyes staring at me from within the flame.

Then something or someone pounded on the ceiling above us. I jumped in my seat.

"What is that?" I blurted out.

Mr. Carlton sighed. "It's just the boiler kicking in and heating up the pipes."

Around me, the kids snickered. I returned my gaze to the lantern on the board. I was sure I saw eyes inside the flames, which grew brighter and brighter. Then the noise stopped and the image was gone.

Dylan uncovered his ears while our teacher droned on about *Frankenstein*. "Victor Frankenstein's monster is a symbol of the folly of humankind seeking knowledge. If you're going to open a door, you may not like what comes through."

I tuned out Mr. Carlton as I stared at the screen, willing the lantern image to return. It did not, and neither did the girl's voice.

After class, I intercepted Dylan at the doorway. "Tell me you saw what I did."

"Shh!" Dylan glanced at the teens walking by then pulled me into the hallway. "Keep your voice down, Kristina. You don't want anyone to think you're crazy."

"I know what I saw, and I'm pretty sure you saw it, too."

He shook his head. "I don't know what you're talking about."

"The lantern and the eyes in the flame," I said.

He began to chew on his lower lip. "Did you also hear the voice?"

I nodded. "What was it?"

"My brother says the school is haunted."

I laughed. "I'm not ten years old, Dylan."

"I didn't believe it at first, either. Thought it was one of those dumb urban legends the ninth graders told to scare the seventh graders. But it definitely looks like this place is haunted."

"What's the story? Let me guess. You say 'Bloody Mary' in front of a mirror five times and she comes to kill you. *Oooo*."

"Hey, I'm just telling you what I've heard."

"Why didn't the others see what we did?"

"I don't know. It's like they can't see what's going on around them. Maybe if their phones were haunted, they might notice. The teachers brush off the flickering lights and weird noises because it's an old school."

"But you heard the sounds from the ceiling, right?" I asked.

He glanced up and nodded.

"So I'm not crazy."

"I'd rather go with being nuts than the other explanation."

"Which is?"

"The ghosts have chosen us," he whispered.

The temperature in the hall seemed to drop a few degrees. Goosebumps popped up all along my exposed forearms. I pulled my green sweater sleeves over my wrists. But curiosity tickled the back of my neck like an itch I needed to scratch.

"You coming?" he asked.

"You go ahead. I'll catch up."

"It's your funeral." He hustled away.

I crept toward the SmartBoard. Maybe there was something behind it, I thought. But the screen seemed to be firmly attached to the wall. I inspected the white screen, searching for a hint or afterimage of the lantern. Nothing.

The noise above picked up again. I stepped back from the screen. The sound grew louder. The screen flickered to life. The image of the lantern returned, clearer than before. The lantern's cap resembled an overturned funnel, marked with the faint impression of a majestic bird spreading its wings.

The lantern's flame grew larger and I could make out the eyes within the fire. The outline of a girl's coffee-coloured face began to come into focus. Her intense gaze stunned me. One eye was blue and the other was green. She had a beauty mark on her right cheek, and she seemed to be mouthing something at me. Part of me wanted to run, but my curiosity rooted my feet to the floor.

I leaned closer and watched her lips. The girl in the flames mouthed the same words again and again: *"Help me."*

2: GHOST STORIES

"**D**ylan! Wait up," I called as I ran toward him in the school parking lot.

"Couldn't stay away from me? I have that effect on people," he said loudly enough for the kids nearby to hear. They ignored him.

"How about you tell me more about the haunted school."

He kicked up his longboard and stuck it under his arm. "Why the sudden interest? Did you see something else in the classroom?"

"Did anyone die here? Maybe a girl?"

He walked away from the oblivious kids. "Don't mind us; we're just going to hunt the chupacabra." Every kid was glued to a screen.

"What can you tell me about the history of this place?" I asked.

"Bet the building doesn't look anything like your old school."

"Not at all. It's more like a fortress."

"My brother said this used to be a convent

where nuns lived. In 1918, there was an epidemic—an outbreak. They called it the Spanish Flu."

"I've heard of that. Millions of people died from it."

He nodded. "The sisters turned their convent into a makeshift hospital, but a lot of flu patients died. Even some of the nuns. My brother said the top floor was where they kept the sickest patients."

"The thumping comes from there."

"My brother says the dead relive their last moments of agony for all time. They're banging on the walls or floor for mercy."

"You believe this story?"

"It beats the principal's explanation that old ducts are expanding and contracting."

"What about the screen acting up?"

"The teachers chalk it up to old equipment. If you haven't figured it out by now, we're not the richest of schools. Things kind of calmed down for a couple of months, but they started up again just a while ago."

"When?"

He shrugged. "Right before you showed up."

"You're joking."

"Nope."

"What's on the fourth floor now?"

"The school uses it for storage, but some of

the kids say they've seen hospital beds stacked up in the corner. I wouldn't be surprised if there was a decayed body up there."

"You've got some imagination," I said. "I don't believe in ghost stories, Dylan."

"You heard the pounding and you saw the eyes in the flame. One blue and one green, right?"

I nodded.

"How do you explain all of this?"

Unfortunately, I had nothing to offer. "Give me time."

"Okay. See you tomorrow," Dylan said. He tossed his longboard down, hopped on, and rolled away.

I headed to the bus stop and back to the apartment my mom and I now shared.

My mom's apartment was tiny compared to our old home. The living room with its pullout sofa doubled as my bedroom. I tossed my backpack on the cushions then fired up my laptop. We'd downsized our belongings to fit into this one-bedroom apartment after my dad left us with a pile of bills and my mom decided to go back to school.

On the night table beside the couch, I placed my Eeyore stuffy right behind the paperweight my grandmother had given me when I was five. The carp-shaped jade trinket was my only reminder of Lao Lao. She had told me the charm would help me overcome whatever problems I faced. Whenever I needed to find hope, all I had to do was rub the jade fish. Beside the carp, my multi-coloured hair elastics dangled from a jewellery tree in the shape of the Olympic rings. Each elastic had come from one of my best friends. Green for Gloria. Purple for Rachel. Red and blue both came from Jen because she was my very best friend. And the white came from Sasha. I wished my friends were here right now.

I rested my fingers on the keyboard. The image on the lantern had seemed familiar. I brought up a search engine and typed the word "lantern."

The first page showed a bunch of camping lamps. I cycled through search entry after search entry, but nothing matched. I entered the words "old-fashioned lanterns." Kerosene lanterns popped up on the screen, but none looked right. I scrolled down the search entries, finally giving up when pictures of "Green Lantern" popped up.

I slumped back. Where had I seen the image on the top of the lantern before? The bird appeared as if it were taking flight—almost as if it were rising from the flame. A smile spread across my face. I had seen it on a *Harry Potter* novel. I typed "phoenix" and "lantern."

The screen filled with entries about a legendary bird rising from the ashes of its old self, being reborn from flames. I pulled my hair out of the ponytail, sifting out the tangles. None of the search images matched the lantern. What did a phoenix have to do with the girl in the flames or the noise from the school's fourth floor?

The rattle of keys grabbed my attention. I closed the laptop and stood up as Mom opened the door. She tilted to one side from the briefcase and bags of groceries in one hand. I rushed to help right her.

"You're home early," I said.

"And hello to you," she replied.

"Hi, Mom."

"How was school?"

"The usual."

She smiled. "We went from 'it sucks' to 'I hate it' to 'the usual' in three days. I think we're making progress, unless 'the usual' means it sucked."

I rolled my eyes as I set the bags on the tiny kitchen counter.

"Anything interesting happen?" she asked.

"I met this guy. Dylan."

She narrowed her gaze.

"Not that kind of guy. He's the first person who's actually talked to me."

"Talking is good."

"He said the school was haunted."

Now it was Mom's turn to roll her eyes. "Oh, Kristina, don't tell me this is another one of your excuses for why you can't go to school here."

"No, it isn't, but now that you bring it up, I have to take the bus to this school anyway. It'd be just as easy to take the number 12 to my old school on the south side."

"Come on, Kristina. Give it another month. Besides, you know what to do if you see a ghost. Remember?"

"Mom," I said, shaking my head.

"Maybe if you invite Dylan over, I could tell him all about it."

"He's not coming over. Ever. And you can never talk about my ghost-busting days."

"You were so cute, peeking in the closets for the ghost."

"Lao Lao scared me with that stupid story about spirits never leaving their homes."

"Then she had to tell you the way to drive them out. You were determined to find our house ghost. I was cleaning up your spit from every piece of furniture for a week."

"You were so mad at her for telling me to spit at the ghosts. I think that's when I learned how to swear in Cantonese."

"Well, I'm glad you grew out of that phase," she said, then fell silent.

"I wish she was still here," I said.

Mom hugged me. I didn't want her to let go.

The next day, I searched for Dylan in the schoolyard. No sign of him outside. I didn't peg him as a keener, but he might have gone into the library to get some studying done. I headed into the school. Too early for classes to begin, the main corridor was deserted. At the far end, one of the locker doors appeared to be bulging. As I walked closer, the blue paint on the metal door began to blister and burn, turning black from the edges in.

My stomach lurched from a stench that now wafted in the air. The entire hallway reeked of rotten eggs and old Chinese takeout. The door turned completely black except for the stencilled outline of a word: "Trapped."

A pounding began; growing louder and more frantic until I thought the door was going to fly off its hinges. Then nothing.

I gingerly reached out and touched the metal. To my surprise, it was cold, almost icy. I hooked the sleeve of my green sweater over my fingers and opened the locker. A hand grabbed my shoulder.

"Oh!" I squealed.

"What's up, Kristina?" he asked. "Hey, why are you trying to get into my locker?"

"This is yours?"

He nodded.

"The ghost left you a message," I said. I swung the door closed, but the message and the blackened paint were gone.

"This was burnt black," I said.

"What did the message say?"

"Trapped."

"Let's take a look," Dylan said, swinging the door open.

In the locker, textbooks were stacked on top of each other like collapsed Jenga tiles. The waistband of a smelly pair of gym shorts poked out from within the pile. I recoiled from the "boy's locker" smell, but nothing about it was out of the ordinary.

"Something or someone was banging inside it," I insisted.

Dylan examined the inside walls. "Well, there's nothing here now, Kristina."

He shoved his dirty shorts under the books.

"I'm starting to believe in what you were saying yesterday," I said.

"Wish I could transfer out of here," Dylan said. "This place creeps me out."

"You know that lantern we saw on the screen?"

"Yeah?"

"I think I know what the decoration on it is," I said.

"Seriously? What?"

"I think it's some kind of phoenix."

"A what?"

"According to legend, it's a firebird. A creature that is reborn out of its own ashes."

"A bird that catches on fire. What's that have to do with an old school?"

"I don't know, but the fact that your locker had burned black means I might not be far off the mark."

"What does a phoenix have to do with the flu?" he asked.

"I'm just telling you what I found on the Internet, Dylan."

The buzzer rang. Dylan tugged at his hemp bracelet. "You know the only way to know for sure what's going on here is to check out the fourth floor."

A centipede of dread crawled up my spine. "You want to go to the source?"

"At least we'll find out what's going on. What do you think?"

"If this were a horror movie, we'd be the first victims," I said.

He grinned. "Good thing, this isn't a horror movie. Come on. End of the day. Are you up for it?"

"Hmm, do homework or go get killed. Decisions, decisions, decisions."

He cocked his head to the side. "You in or you out?"

I nodded. "Fine. Let's do it."

3: The Fourth Floor

The last class of the day seemed to drag on forever. Our math teacher droned on about quadratic equations with the monotonous rhythm of a hypnotist trying to put a person to sleep. I almost fell under his spell twice. Two desks over, a guy's head bobbed up and down as he drifted in and out of consciousness. He had a severe case of sleepy-baby head. The classroom clock ticked off the agonizing minutes to the end of the day. In five minutes, I'd be saying goodbye to boring math problems and saying hello to the fourth floor.

As the seconds counted down, I started to lose my nerve. Part of me wanted to slink out of the school before Dylan could find me. I'd come up with some kind of lie about why I didn't show up. Another part of me was like the girl who discovered a whitehead on her nose. I knew I shouldn't pop it, but the urge was too great.

After what seemed like an eternity, the

dismissal bell rang, and I jumped out of my desk. In the hallway, kids stampeded for the exit, but I headed to the stairwell, where Dylan played with the wheels of his longboard.

"You sure you want to do this, Kristina?"

"You scared?"

"No. Let's go." He ushered me up the steps.

The second floor was cleared of students. The custodian wheeled a shop vacuum out of her office, ignoring us as she listened to her iPod. A couple of teachers worked in their classrooms, but the corridor was empty.

"Well, no turning back now," Dylan said, leading the way to the third floor. He stopped before the stairwell to the fourth floor.

The wide staircase ended at a landing, then another flight doubled back and up to the top of the school.

"Ladies first." He waved at the stairs.

I tried to swallow, but my mouth was suddenly dry. I didn't really believe in ghosts anymore, but without any logical explanation for the strange things happening at the school, I couldn't discount the flu story. Step by step, we climbed the first flight of stairs. The floor groaned under my runners.

About halfway up, I reached out to steady myself on the thick wooden banister running up the stairs. Deep grooves cut into the wood, and the image of someone dragging their fingernails across the railing popped into my head.

Beside me, Dylan's breathing grew more rapid. His face was shiny and he tugged on his hemp bracelet so hard I thought he was going to rip it off.

We finally reached the landing below where the fourth floor awaited us.

Dust kicked up from our shoes as we inched past the window that overlooked the almost empty parking lot below. I surveyed the top of the next flight and what I saw made the hair on the back of my neck stand straight up.

A lone light bulb illuminated a set of double doors with glass windows protected by a wire mesh. A thick chain coiled around the handles and a padlock held it in place.

"What could be on the other side of the doors so that they need to be chained shut?" Dylan asked.

We climbed the final flight of stairs. A chilly breeze wafted down and goosebumps popped up along my arms. I wanted to run down the steps, but we had come too far now. Dylan's hand trembled as he grabbed the railing and took the next step.

Suddenly, the light burned out with a pop,

plunging the landing into dark shadows. We glanced at each other.

"You sure you want to keep going?"

I almost said no. Instead, I asked, "What about you? Are you scared?"

"No," he squeaked.

"Then let's see what's up there."

For a second, neither of us moved. Then a pounding from behind the door broke the spell. I started to retreat. Dylan grabbed my wrist, his fingers digging into my skin.

"Tell me you heard that," he said.

"Yes," I barely whispered.

Then under the crack of the door, a yellow glow began to emit from the space beyond.

"Someone's up there," I said.

His fingers dug deeper. I winced and tried to pull away.

"Sorry," he said, relaxing his grip.

I took a step up and he followed. The glow grew brighter as we approached. The pounding stopped. I tried not to make any noise as I crept up, hanging on to the banister for balance. The wood was warm, almost hot against my hand.

When we reached the top, Dylan crouched to keep his head under the window. I copied him. He set his longboard on the dusty floor.

"What are you going to do?" I asked.

He placed his finger to his lips then he reached for the padlock. He tugged it once, but the lock held tight. The chains slid along the handle once, making a faint *kerchunk*. He froze. I listened for any signs of life on the other side of the door.

An eternity ticked by. No movement or sound. I slid up the door. Dylan grabbed my sleeve.

"I'll be careful," I whispered, shaking off his clammy hand.

I pressed my shoulder against the wooden door and slid up to the window. My eyes widened. I had expected maybe to see a dusty storage area or maybe an old hospital, but what I saw had nothing to do with schools or hospitals.

"Impossible!" I whispered.

The room was too big to fit for the space it occupied. The ceilings reached up at least another three storeys and the chamber itself stretched well beyond what I knew to be the school's walls. Within the vast space was a museum collection of ancient artefacts and books. In the centre, the glow came from a lantern.

"What do you see?" Dylan asked.

I grabbed him by the back of his shirt and hauled him up.

He gasped. "That's not possible. There's no way this can be here."

I agreed, but the only way to know if this

was an illusion or not was to go in. The padlock stood between the lantern and us. I tested one of the door handles and the door creaked open a few inches until the chain caught.

"Careful," Dylan said. "Someone could hear us."

"Hold on to the door."

He took hold of the edge and jerked the door open just wide enough for me to squeeze through.

"Dylan, keep holding it open."

I squeezed under the chain and through the opening. The door scraped against my stomach and back, but I wriggled into the room. I climbed to my feet and looked around the magnificent chamber.

Not a speck of dust anywhere. Heavy stone archways bracketed the perimeter and gargoyles perched near the ceiling. Twisted staircases rose from the floor, going nowhere and back. They zigzagged to an invisible second level but ended before they reached any landing. One staircase doubled back on itself and started where it began. The steps reminded me of the bizarre, ever-changing staircases in Hogwarts, but these never ended.

"Little help here," Dylan grunted.

I heaved my weight against the door and managed to widen the gap just enough so he could squirm through. Once inside, he tucked his shirt into his pants.

"Wow," he said. "What do you think all of this is? Maybe the nuns were hiding loot."

"They would have taken this stuff away when the school took over."

Dylan stepped toward the lantern.

"Careful," I hissed, following him.

The flame beckoned me, and the vast room seemed to glow brighter. Above, crystal chandeliers bounced the light around, bathing the entire chamber in an orange glow.

I peered at the lantern and noticed an inscription engraved on the grimy metal nameplate under the phoenix's talons.

A girl's voice whispered in my ears. "Free me."

The flame danced on a wick and seemed to bow to me.

"*Free me...*"

I turned to Dylan who was halfway up one of the strange staircases.

"Did you hear that?" I called after him.

"No. You think someone's here?"

"You don't hear the whispering?"

He shook his head. "Maybe it's the ghosts. They're coming for you, Kristina."

I rolled my eyes and turned back to the

lantern. The flame was dancing wildly now, but there was no opening for a breeze to blow through. How could the flame move on its own like this? When I examined the flame through the glass panel, I noticed the wick appeared to be the end of a long chain that wound around the base of the lantern.

Suddenly, Dylan appeared beside me. I jumped.

"Easy there, slick. It's just me."

"Sorry."

"What do you see?"

I pulled my sleeve over my hand and rubbed the nameplate to reveal the first part of a title: "Flame of—"

Suddenly, the flame jumped from the wick and black smoke poured out from the lantern. The smoke swirled around us, twisting like a boa constrictor until it coiled around Dylan and me several times.

Dylan cried out, "Don't touch the smoke! It's hot."

Somewhere from the upper chambers, a door opened casting a blue light across the room. A silhouette was framed in the doorway.

"Who's there?" a voice called down.

The smoke dispersed from around our bodies and billowed toward the double doors. It flowed under the crack, followed by the hiss of the girl's voice.

"Freedom!"

"Halt!" the man on the stairs shouted.

Dylan grabbed my arm and pulled me toward the doors. "Our cue to leave," he said.

We sprinted toward the exit. I scraped a layer of skin from my forearm as I forced my way through the door Dylan had shoved open for me. Once on the other side, I strained to hold it open for him.

Footsteps echoed in the chamber.

"Move," I hissed.

"I'm trying," Dylan said.

He was about halfway through the door. I glanced through the lattice window. A tall man with a tweed suit and wild, white hair was racing toward us.

Dylan groaned as he pushed himself forward. I grabbed his collar and tried to yank him through the opening. The man was almost on top of us.

"Push!" I shouted.

Dylan yowled in pain as he squeezed through the gap. I shoved the door closed just as the white-haired man reached it. His face filled the window. Then the screech of metal wrenching against itself reverberated in the air.

I shut my eyes and winced at the sound.

When I opened them, there was no sign of the man on the other side of the meshed window.

The chamber was gone, too, replaced with a dusty storage area filled with cardboard boxes.

4: The New Girl

My lungs burned as I chased after Dylan. He slid down the stairwells without even a backward glance, hurtling out of the building and into the open air. Dylan finally stopped when he reached the chain-link fence around the schoolyard. He doubled over and gasped for air.

"Tell me you saw the same thing," he wheezed. "Tell me I'm not crazy."

"You're not crazy."

"The smoke moved like it was alive. How is that even possible?"

"I don't know. Should we tell someone about the storage area?" I asked.

Dylan gulped. "Are you kidding? Who's going to believe us? 'Excuse us, Principal Michaels, but the fourth floor is magically disappearing and reappearing at night. And there's a smoke monster loose in the building.' You think that isn't going to land us in a counsellor's office?"

"I guess you're right," I said. "What do you think it is?"

"I don't know and I don't care. All I know is that I'm going to get my mom to start looking for another school because there's no way I'm sticking around here."

I patted him on the back. "Calm down, Dylan. It's not like you see something like this every day. Besides, what are you going to tell your mom? That you're scared of the fourth floor?"

He straightened up. "You're telling me you're not even a little freaked out by all of this?"

"Of course I am! But I'm also curious. Aren't you?"

"The top of the school is haunted. That's all I need to know."

"We have to find out why."

"Why do you care? You've been at the school for barely a week."

"Yes, but aren't you curious? I can't walk around pretending the fourth floor doesn't exist."

Dylan shrugged. "Truth is, Kristina, it *doesn't* exist."

"You know what I'm trying to say."

"I do, but I don't have to like it."

"Why are you so scared, Dylan?"

"Because we're the only ones who see this

weird crap. We start telling people and it's game over for both of us."

"I'm sure someone else will see it, too," I said doubtfully.

He leaned against a streetlamp. "Kristina, you're not new at life, are you? You know what it's like to be in junior high."

"At least people will notice you now."

"I wanted people to know I was alive, not a freak. We start telling ghost stories, they're going to think we're elementary students. The trolls would make it their mission to humiliate us."

"You're blowing this up."

"Last year, a girl in grade nine got a part in a national commercial. She was small, so she played a girl in the back seat of a car who really needed to go to the bathroom."

"So?"

"Everyone started to make fun of her. They nicknamed her Diaper Denise. A couple of jerks filled her pencil case with crayons and swapped out her textbooks with colouring books. Then someone started taping diapers to her locker. She transferred to another school because the bullying got so bad. Can you imagine what the knuckle-draggers would do to us if they thought we believed in ghosts?"

"Okay, how about this. Tomorrow, we go back up and see if the room comes back," I said.

"If it doesn't, then we just pretend today never happened."

"You're a toddler with her favourite stuffy. You're just not going to let this go, are you?"

"I can do it without you, but it would be a lot better if you were with me."

"Why? So you can shove me to the ghosts?"

I smiled. "If I remember, you were the one I had to catch up to when we ran out of the school. Besides, I think you left your longboard upstairs."

His eyes widened. "Damn it. I can't believe I was that stupid."

"So tomorrow after school, we'll go up, right?"

He smacked his hand against his forehead as he walked away. "Stupid, stupid, stupid."

"Dylan? Tomorrow?"

He kept walking.

That night, I combed the Internet for ghost stories about places that disappeared and reappeared. In an Irish legend, a traveller stumbled across a fairy world where he danced for hours, but when he returned to our world, years had passed. A Slavic myth referred to a phantom island where three brothers lived. The island could appear and disappear. I also found a reference to a legend about Atlantis, an island that was supposed to have been swallowed by the sea. But there wasn't a single story about rooms that mysteriously appeared and disappeared.

Whatever the fourth floor was, it had nothing to do with the usual crop of ghost stories. I closed my laptop and curled up on my sofa bed. I drew my blanket over my shoulder and tried to sleep, but the vision of the smoke haunted me. I swore I heard a girl's voice when the smoke wrapped around me. Her voice echoed like the ringing in my ears I'd get during the ride home after a concert.

I drifted off to sleep with one thought: *Who was free?*

The next day, I tracked down the reluctant Dylan hiding in the cafeteria and convinced him to help me.

"If I go and disappear forever, you'll tell my mom, right?" I said. "But you'll have to walk all the way to my apartment, since your longboard will also be toast."

"Okay, okay. Let's get this over with."

We returned to the fourth floor. Dylan

showed no interest in looking through the lattice windows; instead, he just grabbed his longboard and scurried back down the stairs to the landing to wait for me. I stared through the mesh at the storage room full of cardboard boxes. No sign of the twisting staircases or the bizarre antiques anywhere. I lingered around the doors until the school bell rang then I shuffled down the stairs to join Dylan.

"Anything?" he asked.

I shook my head. "Maybe tomorrow."

The next day, I hoped to catch a glimpse of the fourth floor chamber or the strange smoke, but Dylan refused to come along. He slammed his locker shut.

"You ever hear that saying about what curiosity did to the cat?" he asked. "Killed him dead."

"I'm no cat," I said.

"And I'm not an idiot. Go if you want. Leave me out of it."

"Will you at least stick nearby in case I need help? You can just stand on the stairs."

"No. I'm steering clear of Spook Central. And so should you." He stomped down the hall before I could change his mind.

Alone, I ascended the stairs to the fourth floor that day, and the next one, and the one after. Each time, the storage area remained dusty and unremarkable.

The only strange thing that happened at school was the fact that nothing strange happened at school. The pounding on the ceiling had stopped. The whispering had ceased. Even Mr. Carlton's SmartBoard was working, at least when he didn't accidentally crash the system. For about a week, MacKenzie King School was free of weirdness.

In language arts class, Mr. Carlton wrapped up the novel study of *Frankenstein* in his typical droning fashion. "In my favourite scene, Victor comes face to face with his creation while he is on vacation. The author gives us a short break from the death of Victor's brother. A calm before the storm, as it were, before the monster appears to his creator and pleads for him to create a companion, thus emphasizing the fact that even a monster can have humanity."

Suddenly, I heard pounding. I stiffened. Had the girl in the lantern returned to the fourth floor? I gripped the sides of my desk to keep from bolting out of the classroom to check on the storage area. This time, I wasn't the only one who had heard the noise. All heads turned, not up to the ceiling, but across the room to the door.

Just outside the classroom was a dark-skinned teen in a black leather jacket. Flame tattoos ran up her arms and circled her neck. I barely noticed her silver fingernails because of all the rings she had on every finger. She raised her hand to scratch her nose just under her nose ring. Had I seen her before? She strutted into the room, handed Mr. Carlton a slip of paper, and fixed her gaze on me.

I stiffened. Her eyes! One was blue and the other was green, just like the girl from the lantern.

Mr. Carlton sighed as he read the paper. "Welcome, uh—"

"Niram," she interjected.

"Right. Niram. Take the empty desk beside Kristina." He waved dismissively then returned to scribbling Frankenstein motifs on the whiteboard.

"Is this going to be on the test?" Dylan asked.

A few snickers came from the students within earshot. Thorn the Goth girl refused to laugh, of course. She might have had her sense of humour removed when she hit puberty. She shifted in her seat, sizing up the newest Goth girl at school.

Niram turned to me and cracked a smile. "Hi."

"Hi. I'm Kristina," I answered awkwardly. Her eyes were freaking me out a bit, to be honest.

"Nice to meet you. I feel a bit lost here. Do you think you could help me? Show me around?"

"Uh, sure. I guess."

"I'm in your debt," she said. "Your wishes are my command."

Odd thing to say, I thought. Her voice sounded similar to the girl from the lantern, but I wasn't sure. I pretended not to stare, but I continued to spy on Niram through the rest of Mr. Carlton's lecture. His monotone voice threatened to lull everyone in class to sleep, but I was on high alert.

About ten minutes into the never-ending talk, Niram leaned over and whispered, "I heard Mary Shelley wrote a sequel where Frankenstein's monster kills people with sheer boredom."

I pretended to laugh. Mr. Carlton recapped the motifs on the whiteboard, turning his back on the class. Niram reached into her pocket, pulled out a smartphone, and posed for a pic. She rolled her eyes back and cocked her head to one side as if she were a corpse. She snapped the photo and turned the screen around to show me.

"Nice," I said.

"I did it right, didn't I?" she asked.

"What do you mean?"

"That's how you take a selfie, isn't it?"

I cocked my head to one side. How could she not know? "Um, sure."

"Excellent. Now I'll post it on Facebook."

"No," I answered. "Now you post it on

Instagram. Not Facebook. That's for old people and their cats."

"How do I find In-sta-gram?" she asked.

"I'll show you after class," I said, pointing at Mr. Carlton who started to turn around.

When the dismissal bell rang, I led Niram out into the hall. Thorn was waiting just outside the door. She elbowed Niram to one side.

"Poseur," she muttered and stomped down the hallway.

"Don't mind her," I said. "Thorn's our school crank. She hates being here."

"Why doesn't she just leave?' Niram said.

"Drop out? I think her parents would kill her."

"Ah, she is bound here."

"I guess you could say that," I said. This girl was definitely an odd one, and I started to wonder if she came from the lantern or from another planet. "So where are you from?" I asked.

Niram bowed her head. "You probably haven't heard of it. Akkad."

"Where's that?"

She ignored my question, interjecting her own. "Will you show me this In-sta-gram now?"

"Sure," I said. "Show me your smartphone."

She handed over her phone. Only basic apps were loaded on the phone. The device was almost as new as Niram. I downloaded a few social media apps for her. "Instagram lets you post photos, and people who are your followers will like or comment on them," I explained.

"You have one of these?"

I fished out my smartphone and showed her photos of Mom and me. I had deleted all the ones of Dad.

"She is pretty."

"That's my mom."

"What is the heart for?" Niram asked.

"You click on it if you like the photo."

"And then what?"

"Well, then you take a whole bunch of selfies and see who will notice you. Sometimes, you can get people from another country liking your photos. And sometimes, you can get creeps, so be careful."

"You know, Kristina, in Akkad, if someone helps you, you owe them three... um... the word we use you would not understand. I think it is 'wishes.' Does that make sense?"

I corrected her. "I think you meant favours."

"Thank you. Favours. I owe you three favours. All you have to do is wish for them."

"That's a sweet custom, but I haven't really done anything."

"Then let us take a picture together." Niram held up the phone to take a selfie, but before she could press the button, Dylan photobombed us.

"*Wagggllle*," he said, flashing devil horns.

Niram mimicked him. "*Wagggllle.*"

He raised an eyebrow. "You making fun of me?"

"Isn't that how you say hello to someone new?"

"No," I said. "This is my friend, Dylan. He thinks he's funny."

She laughed. "Yes, he is."

"Don't encourage him," I groaned.

"I like this one, Kristina. Can we keep her?" Dylan offered Niram his hand. "Shake?"

She began to thrash her body around. He laughed and joined her in the body shake fest, which actually attracted the attention of some of the students walking past. Leaning against her locker down the hall, Thorn sniffed and commented to her pack of Goth wannabes, "That's what happens when cousins marry."

Dylan fell silent, but Niram cocked her head to one side. "I have no cousins."

Thorn and the other girls snickered before turning away from Niram as if she were patient zero in a zombie outbreak.

"Don't let them get to you," I said. "Thorn's got some issues."

She sighed. "I'm used to her kind. Now,

Kristina, on to your favours. What would you like me to do for you?"

I waved her off. "Nothing, Niram."

"But your kind always wants something. Surely, you can think of one thing."

"Nope." My kind?

She leaned in a little too close. "Give it some thought. I'm here to serve you."

"Uh, thanks?" I said, flashing Dylan a sideways glance.

Niram gripped my wrist. "Whatever you desire."

Her fingers burned into my flesh. I yanked my arm away.

Dylan knifed his body between us: "Get a selfie of the three of us, Niram."

She pulled out her smartphone. "Kristina, do you wish to be in the picture?"

"No, you two go ahead." I rubbed my wrist where Niram had grabbed me. There were no marks, but the skin still felt hot to the touch.

5: THE VAULT

At lunch, I veered away from the cafeteria and grabbed Dylan in the hallway. I wanted to share my suspicions about the similarities between the ghost image and the new girl at school. He was all ears.

"They both have different coloured eyes," I said.

"I'll give you that, but she touched you. Can ghosts do that?"

"I don't know, but her hand was hot like the smoke."

"So what's the connection between her and the lantern on the fourth-floor-that-isn't-there?"

"Maybe she was trapped inside and we set her free."

"Okay, let's say you're right. What does she want from you?"

"Why do you think she wants something from me?"

"Because she tagged along behind you like

a lonely puppy all day," he said. "And because she's coming up right now."

Niram strolled toward us. She waved to get my attention, sidling past Thorn and her group of Goth girls.

"Kristina, Kristina! Wait up."

Thorn waved her hands in the air, mockingly. "Kristina, Kristina. Wait up!"

The Goth girls chuckled. Niram stopped and turned to the kids. Thorn unclipped the leather dog collar from around her neck and offered it up. "Niram, looks like you need this more than me. You'll just need a leash."

"Why would you give me this?"

Thorn blinked innocently. "That's because you're Kristina's dog." she said with exaggerated slowness, as if she were talking to a toddler.

Thorn tossed the collar at Niram's feet. "Fetch."

Niram murmured. "You're mocking me."

The Goth girls started to bark.

"*Arf, arf, mon petit chien,*" Thorn said.

Niram's nostrils flared. The hallway seemed to grow hotter. For a moment, I thought I could almost see waves of heat flowing down the cramped corridor.

Apparently, I wasn't the only one feeling warm. Thorn's posse began to shift uncomfortably and fan themselves.

Niram glared at Thorn. "I've done you no wrong. Why are you doing this?"

"You know, when your mouth's closed, you're kind of pretty," Thorn said. "You should keep it closed more often."

Niram narrowed her gaze. The hallway felt as if someone had just opened an oven door. Hot air blasted my face. I rushed over to escort Niram away from Thorn, but when I touched her shoulder I nearly burned my fingers. The other students gathered around us.

"Looks like your master has come to get you," Thorn said. "Good girl."

The kids laughed.

"Why don't you leave her alone, Thorn?" I said.

Thorn sized me up. "And what are you going to do about it?"

Dylan butted in between us. "Absolutely nothing, but I'm sure Principal Michaels might."

"Losers talk," she shot back.

The students murmured in agreement.

"Well, it looks like you've been doing most of the talking, so that would make you a..." I quipped.

The tide turned on Thorn as all but her posse laughed. She sneered as she strode forward.

"Stick your nose in my business again. I dare you."

"What's the matter, Thorn? You afraid everyone will figure out you're a fraud when a real Goth girl shows up?" I said, glancing at Niram.

Thorn pushed me. The crowd *ooed*, sensing a fight. I wasn't about to give them one.

"Say that again and we'll see who's a fraud," Thorn threatened.

"I just wish you'd leave me alone."

Niram muttered something behind me. I thought she said, "As you command." The hallway suddenly grew very hot as if a fire were burning behind me. I started to turn around, but the fire alarm distracted me. The blare filled the hallway. Kids covered their ears.

Suddenly, a sprinkler sprayed water right over Thorn and her group. They squealed as the water spit on them, making their black makeup run down their cheeks. Then the other sprinklers tripped, and water rained down on everyone. People scattered for the main doors, but Niram didn't budge. Steam seemed to rise from her body, but Dylan and the throng of kids swept me away before I could be sure.

Outside, wet students wrung out hoodies and fanned smartphones. The teachers had gathered outside as well, trying to round everyone up into their assigned fire drill formations. The head count began. The only one missing was Niram. I scanned the schoolyard for her, but she was nowhere to be seen.

Finally, I spotted her slipping out one of the side doors. I could have sworn she was completely dry.

After nearly an hour, Principal Michaels shouted at us that the sprinkler system had been tripped by some kind of false reading. She waved us back into the building. "Go to your block five classes," she ordered.

The rest of the afternoon was a mess. Everyone chattered about the sprinklers going off. Strangely, Thorn and her friends avoided me. In the hallway, they veered around me as if they were sidling past a sinkhole. Even in class, the girls moved their desks away and refused to make any eye contact.

At the end of the day, I decided to make amends with Thorn. I feared she might be hatching some kind of revenge plot, but when I approached her, she backed off. The closer I tried to get, the more she scrambled away. She almost seemed afraid of me.

"Thorn, I just want to talk."

She shook her head. "You said to leave you alone." She ran down the hallway, as I just stared after her in bewilderment.

Behind me, Dylan let out a low whistle. "Looks

like there's a new boss in the game and her name is Kristina. How did you scare off Thorn?"

"I didn't. That's the thing. She's been acting like this since the sprinklers went off."

"Wonder why?" he asked, scratching his head.

"This might sound weird, but I think it might have something to do with Niram. Just before the sprinklers went off, I thought I heard her say something."

"What did she say?" Dylan asked.

"It made no sense. Something about it being 'my command.' I've been wondering about it all day." I paused for a moment and looked him in the eye. "I think we should go back to the fourth floor."

"You're crazy. No way am I going back up there."

"When the sprinklers sprayed on Niram, she started to steam. And when she came out of the school, she was bone dry."

"But everyone in the hall got blasted with water. How could she stay dry?" he asked.

"I'm not sure, but the answer is in the lantern. Are you in or out, Dylan?"

He sighed. "I think I should leave a will just in case we don't come back."

The landing was dark as we climbed toward the fourth floor. The bulb had burnt out. I fished my smartphone out of my back pocket and turned on the flashlight app. Blue light cut through floating dust particles as we tiptoed up the second flight of stairs. Dylan grabbed my arm.

"The light. If someone's up there, they'll know we're here," he said.

"Yes, but the light keeps us from breaking our necks."

"Good point."

Once we reached the landing and peered through the mesh windows, all we saw was the storage area—again. Dylan sighed with relief.

"Okay, it's still gone. Let's go back down."

"Hold on, Dylan. Maybe going past the doors is what triggers the room to return."

"No, definitely not."

"Or maybe we have to recreate what we did the day we found the room. I think you pulled on the lock. Do that again."

"You sure about this?"

"Do it."

He obeyed. The chain rattled against the handles. I peered through the lattice grate of the window. Nothing changed. This was getting us nowhere fast. I pulled on the door and widened the gap.

"Dylan, stay here. If I disappear, you can go for help."

"No arguments from me," he said, grabbing the edge of the door.

"Hang on to this and give me some light." I handed him my smartphone.

Dylan held the phone over my head with his free hand. I squeezed through the narrow opening. A film of dust coated my hands and knees.

"Okay, I'm in. Give me my phone back."

He passed the device through the gap. I held it up, casting light over the large cardboard boxes. I pointed the light at the creaky wooden floor. Not a single footprint here. This place hadn't been used in ages.

I opened one of the closest boxes and nearly gagged from the stench that wafted up from the mouldy textbooks inside.

Each box contained another forgotten relic of the school's past, but they couldn't compare to the antiques of the other room. I decided to leave and headed back to the exit.

"Did you find anything?" Dylan asked.

"A lot of mould and dust."

"Maybe Niram doesn't want us to find the room," he said. "If she was trapped in the lantern, maybe she wants to stay out."

We headed down the flight of stairs—Dylan leading the way. Before turning the corner onto the next landing, I glanced back at the doors, hoping the room would return. Nothing. I turned to go down the rest of the stairwell and slammed into Dylan's back.

"Whoa, what's wrong?" I asked.

"We've reached level 2, I think," Dylan said.

At the bottom of the next set of stairs was a vast room. Above us, a mural of angels covered a domed ceiling. Around the perimeter, marble archways lined the walls. Behind me, there was nothing but air. The school was nowhere to be found.

At the bottom of the staircase, the tall man with wild, white hair waved us down. "There's only one way to go and that's this way."

"Who are you?" I asked.

The man smiled. "I'm Mr. Grimoire, the keeper of the vault."

6: Grimoire's Tale

Dylan and I perched on a red couch in the centre of the vault while Grimoire poured tea into bone-white teacups on a silver tray. Above, stone gargoyles kept watch over us. Their gazes seemed to pierce my skull. If I could spot an exit, I would have bolted, but the room was nothing but an obstacle course of artefacts, crazy staircases, and long, stone-arched windows. Through the windows I could see a starry night sky and I wondered how long we had been in the vault.

"Where are we?" I asked.

"I'm the one who should be asking the questions," he replied sternly. "How did you gain access to my vault?"

"You call this a vault?" Dylan said. "Looks more like a garage sale."

"Choose your next words carefully, because they may be your last," Grimoire warned.

Dylan fell silent.

"You know you're not supposed to be in our school," I said.

He picked up a silver spoon and stirred his cup of tea. "If we are talking about intrusions, I believe you're standing on a rather unstable ground, considering you've been traipsing through my collection."

"Is this a museum?" I asked.

"A museum is a collection of a record of a civilization meant to be shared with the public. A vault is a collection meant to be kept from the prying eyes of the curious and only to be shared with those who are invited, which brings me to my first question. Who are you and how did you get in here?"

"I'm Dylan and this is my friend, Kristina."

"And if you tell us where *here* is, we might be able to tell you how we got here," I said.

"You're where no one will be able to find you, should that be my decision."

"If you wanted to kill us, you would have already done it," I said. "Only movie villains take the time to talk to their enemies before they do them in."

He sipped his tea. "You are keen. I loathe violence, but that doesn't mean I don't have other means of loosening your tongues. Tea?" He waved at the two other teacups on the silver tray.

"What's in it?" I asked. "Truth serum? Poison?"

"Oolong," he replied. "If you talk, I might even be able to find some scones and jam."

Dylan perked up. "Okay, here's the deal. We went to check out the fourth floor of our school last week, and found your weird place where the storage area should have been. Then today, we went up again, but this time your vault showed up at the bottom of the stairs when we were coming down from the fourth floor."

The tall man turned to me. "Is that how you found my vault?"

"Pretty much. Random coincidence."

"I don't subscribe to chance. Tell me, why the curiosity about the fourth floor?"

Dylan asked, "Weren't you supposed to give us scones and jam?"

"Ah yes, my manners are lacking." Grimoire reached under the table and pulled out a basket. He peeled the red-and-white checkered cloth from the top of the basket to reveal steaming scones and a small pot of red jam.

Dylan smacked his lips like a cat before dinner and held out his hand.

Grimoire hesitated handing over the basket. "One more question. While you were here, did you handle anything?"

"No, sir," Dylan lied.

"You see, it seems that one of my artefacts has been disturbed, and it's given me quite some cause for concern."

"Is it the lantern?" I asked.

Grimoire lowered the basket and fixed a steely-eyed stare at me. "What do you know of the lantern?"

"It's why we tried to find your vault again," I said.

"Did either of you touch it?"

Dylan flashed me a sideways glance and I fiddled with my napkin.

"Uh, sort of," I answered.

Grimoire handed the basket to Dylan. "You'll need sustenance if you are to survive what comes next."

Dylan's mouth dropped open. "I think I just lost my appetite."

"What's coming next?" I asked. "Are we in danger?"

"Not from me. My apologies. This must seem rather overwhelming. Let's start from the beginning. I'm Mr. Grimoire, the keeper of the vault. I protect the contents and keep intruders at bay."

"Not doing a very good job so far," Dylan murmured.

"Yes, it would seem that my security is strangely lax these days. The vault is kept secret by a simple illusion. To most people, the vault should appear as nothing more than a storage room at the top of an old school. This disguise has served me well for many years, but something has changed, and I don't know why. I suspect it has something to do with the two of you. Now, which one of you came into contact with the lantern?"

I sheepishly looked at Mr. Grimoire. "I didn't mean to. I wanted to read the nameplate, so I rubbed off the dust."

"Then you're headed for a storm of misery."

I stiffened.

"Not from me. From the lantern's occupant."

Dylan shot me a look.

"Don't you mean *prisoner*?" I asked.

Grimoire picked up his teacup and took a sip. "An interesting choice of word. How did you come to that conclusion?"

"Dylan and I saw her face in our school, and I heard her begging to be free," I said. "Who is she?"

"Did you not see the name on the lantern?" he asked.

"No, smoke came flying out before I could rub off the dust on the nameplate," I said.

"Then now would be an appropriate time to learn the truth," Grimoire said, beckoning us to follow him to the lantern.

The phoenix engraving on the upside-down funnel stared at me as I drew nearer. The nameplate in the talons read: "Flame of..." but the rest was still covered in grime. Grimoire drew a white silk handkerchief from his breast pocket and wiped away the grime. I gasped.

"It's not possible."

Dylan grabbed my arm. "You can't be serious."

The inscription read, "Flame of Niram."

7: Flame of Niram

"**N**iram! We saw her in the school. She's the new student."

Grimoire tapped the lantern glass. "This is a vessel designed to hold one of the most dangerous mischief makers in our civilized world. You are now bound to her, Kristina."

"How?"

"By the terms of the contract. Niram may seem to be a girl, but she's nothing of the sort. She's an elemental."

"A what?" Dylan asked.

Grimoire stood in front of me and placed his handkerchief back into his pocket. "Tell me. Do you know the story of Aladdin and the Lamp?"

I nodded. "It's a story about a boy who set a genie free from a magic lamp."

"Oh, yeah. And he got three wishes," Dylan added. "Wait. You're telling us that Kristina set a genie free? Does she get wishes?"

"Please, it's not *genie*," Grimoire corrected.

"We call these creatures *djinns*."

Dylan stood up. "I don't care what you call them. I don't believe in fairy tales."

"Not a fairy tale. Folklore. Tales told to warn us away from danger. In this case, the tale is a warning never to set the djinn free."

"Kristina, this guy's lying."

"Dylan's right. There's no such thing as djinns or genies or whatever you call them," I said.

"Then see for yourselves what you're up against." Grimoire motioned us to follow him to a display case near the centre of the room. Mounted inside, a brass lamp glistened in the light. Like the lantern, this artefact had a phoenix engraved on the side.

"Now that's the kind of lamp that would hold a djinn," Dylan joked.

"Observe," Grimoire said. He tapped on the glass case three times.

"Let me sleep," boomed a voice from within. The glass case vibrated.

Grimoire knocked again.

"Leave me to my rest," the deep voice sounded.

"A moment is all I ask."

"I owe you nothing."

Grimoire sighed and placed his hands on a large wheel crank at the base of the display case.

"Must I resort to this every time?"

"You wouldn't dare."

He turned the crank to the left. Inside the case, small vents opened. Then puffs of steam rose from the slits.

"What is that?" Dylan asked.

"I'm merely adjusting the temperature for my guest."

"I'm not coming out," the voice boomed.

Dylan nudged me. "It's probably just a speaker set in the lamp."

Grimoire turned the crank one more time. Frost crystallized on the inside of the glass.

The lamp voice whined. "Enough. Enough. It's freezing in here."

"Prepared to come out now?"

"Yes, yes, yes."

Grimoire spun the crank in the other direction. Slowly, the ice crystals melted into water droplets that rolled down the glass and pooled around the lamp. Black smoke puffed out of the lamp spout and swirled around the inside of the case. The puddle evaporated almost instantaneously. Then the smoke took the shape of a purple-faced bald man's head. Scars cut across the top of his head and his nose was curved almost like a beak. One of his eyes was blue and the other was green.

"What do you want, Grimoire?" the djinn asked.

"Your daughter has escaped."

"Excellent! Finally. Tell me how she did it."

Grimoire shook his head. "That knowledge had best be kept secret."

"You can't blame an elemental for trying."

"Kristina, Dylan. This is Lapulis Azure. He is the original elemental."

The creature's head expanded to fill the entire glass case. "Mortals, I'm going to bite off your puny heads and suck the marrow out of your bones. Now, come here!"

Dylan jumped behind me and yelped. I shut my eyes. Laughter followed. I opened my eyes. The head was smaller and the creature was still inside the case.

"Can't blame a djinn for trying," the purple-faced head said.

Grimoire rapped on the display case. "We're perfectly safe as long as this is intact. Enchanted glass. This is what holds the djinn in place, much like the lantern glass. He is free to come in and out of his lamp, which has all the comforts of his home, but unless someone rubs the glass he remains inside the case."

"I don't know what to believe right now," I said.

Grimoire ignored Dylan and rested his hand on my shoulder. "Young lady, I know all of this sounds rather fantastic, but you have unleashed a fire elemental."

"Is Dylan right about the wishes?" I asked.

"Didn't Niram tell you?"

I shook my head. "The smoke wrapped around us and then flew out when you came into the vault."

"What about when you met her in school?" Grimoire asked.

"No. Wait a minute, she said something about a custom she had where she owed me three favours."

Lapulis Azure laughed. "She's even more clever than her father. I couldn't be prouder."

Grimoire stroked his chin. "Ah, I see her ploy. Kristina, djinns are honoured-bound to their contracts, but they are also deceptive beings. She's told you about the contract, but in a way that only technically fulfills the terms. She was trying to trick you into squandering the wishes before you even knew you had them."

"What happens when she grants all the wishes?" Dylan asked.

"Then Niram is free to wreak havoc on the world. She could bring total destruction upon entire civilizations simply on a whim and kill

69

those who dare to oppose her."

I began to hyperventilate. "I think I already made a wish."

"What?"

"Dylan, you remember Thorn, right? I wished she'd leave us alone, and now she runs from me."

Grimoire grabbed my elbow. "Think carefully, Kristina. Did you ask for anything else?"

I searched my memory for anything I said to Niram. I drew a blank. "I don't think so."

"Then she is still bound to you."

Dylan cocked his head to one side. "Hey, why don't you just wish her back into the lantern."

"Not that simple," Grimoire explained. "That is the one wish she is not obliged to grant. You must outfox a djinn, which is no easy task. She will resort to almost any means to get you to squander your wishes. If there is a loophole, she'll squeeze through it."

"Why doesn't she just kill Kristina?" Dylan asked.

I flashed him a stink eye.

"Sorry."

"It's a fair question, Dylan," Grimoire said. "In the same way, you can't wish her back into the lantern or wish for more wishes, she can't cause you harm directly or indirectly."

"Then how do we get her back into the lantern?" I asked.

Grimoire tapped the display case and stared down at the purple face. "Old nemesis, you know your daughter. What are her weaknesses?"

"Why should I tell you?"

"Because I may have to utilize liquid nitrogen, and I'm afraid she may not have your constitution."

"Not a concern of mine. She's her own elemental now."

"You would leave her to die?" I asked. "How could you? You're her father!"

"Why should I care about her?"

The djinn's comment ripped off the scab over my own heart. My father had said practically the same thing just before he left Mom. Thinking I was asleep in the next room, they argued about getting a divorce. She had asked if he wanted to share custody of me, and his answer had left a permanent wound.

Grimoire tsked at the purple head. "Surely, you must have some concern for her. You two are the last of the known fire elementals."

"My daughter can take care of herself. She learned from the best after all."

"You heartless jerk," I said. "It's your own daughter."

"Ah, guilt. You know, that is a human emotion I have never understood. Just like remorse or fear. And I can see the waves of it coming off you, little one."

I wondered if my dad was one of the djinn because he never seemed to show any remorse for leaving.

"This one's going to be of no assistance at all," Grimoire concluded. "You can go."

"Always a displeasure, Grimoire." Lapulis Azure burst into a cloud of smoke and retreated into the lamp spout. Just like that, he was gone.

Dylan examined the display case, wide-eyed and curious. Then he stiffened. "Wait a minute. What happens if Kristina doesn't make the three wishes?"

I don't know which was worse: the expression on Grimoire's face or the answer he gave: "Then everyone Kristina holds dear is in serious danger. A djinn will put everyone's lives at risk to force Kristina to use up her remaining two wishes."

8: THE SECOND WISH

We spent hours debating in the vault and made no progress about how to trap Niram. Dylan and I pitched ideas on how to trick her back into the lantern while Grimoire shot down every proposal.

"Hey, how about we say her dad got sucked into the lamp?" Dylan suggested. "We tell her she's the only one who can save him."

"Except Niram knows full well that eternal imprisonment is part of an elemental's fate," Grimoire said. "Plus, I don't sense a close bond between the two."

I offered another solution. "We disguise the lantern and I make a wish that she could go inside it."

"Except you can't wish for that," Grimoire pointed out. "You would have to trick her to go into the disguised lantern."

"How about Kristina pretends like she doesn't believe Niram can turn into smoke and gets her to prove it? Then we get a vacuum cleaner to suck up the smoke."

Grimoire said nothing for the longest time. I leaned forward waiting to hear him shoot Dylan down with the constant 'except' interjection. I looked to Dylan, cracking a small smile.

"Except you'd have to make sure the lantern could fit into the vacuum," Grimoire said. "And if you put the lantern in, it will block up the suction and the vacuum won't work at all."

Right about now, I hated the word 'except.'

Dylan pulled at his hair. "I give up."

"Except, we don't have to use the entire lantern," Grimoire added.

I sat up. "What do you mean?"

"It's the glass that is enchanted. The rest of the lantern is just a housing unit. We could take one of the panes and attach it to the vacuum, turning it into the new prison. Yes, this just might work."

Dylan clapped his hands. "Now we just need to find a decent vacuum. I don't suppose you have one in the vault."

"I'm sorry to disappoint you, but I auctioned off all my household items just last week."

"Really?" Dylan said. "Oh. You were being sarcastic."

Grimoire tapped his finger against his nose.

"There's one in the custodian's office," I said.

"Great, I'll go get it," Dylan offered. "You stay here."

"Hey, I'm not a princess waiting to be rescued. I'll come with you."

"Not a wise option," Grimoire said. "Niram is after you."

"You said she'd use my friends. Dylan will be in more danger than me," I argued.

"Then how about Mr. Grimoire goes out and gets the vacuum. Niram doesn't care about him."

"I'm afraid you're wrong, lad. I was the one who imprisoned her. She'd burn down the school if she knew I was out there."

"Well how did you do it the first time? Maybe we can repeat it," I said.

"I made a bargain with her. I said she could go free if she could calculate the final digit of pi. If she couldn't do it, she had to go back into the lantern."

Dylan shook his head. "That's impossible. Pi never ends."

I beamed. "I could use that as one of my wishes!"

"Except you can only fool a djinn once with a trick like that. I'm sure in the time she's been imprisoned she's had enough time to figure out a loophole, and you really only have one shot at it."

"Then how are we supposed to get the vacuum?" Dylan asked.

"We need to find out where Niram is to see if it is safe for Kristina to leave."

"You mean before Kristina and I leave the vault. I need to get home before my parents start to worry."

"Okay, we find out where Niram is and then we make our plans from there," I said. "Where would she go, Mr. Grimoire?"

"She's a djinn. If she wanted, she could sleep on the moon."

"But where do you think she would want to stay?" Dylan asked.

"I couldn't tell you for certain. I imagine someplace warm."

I cracked a smile. "Wait! I set her up on Instagram. Maybe she's been posting photos. We might be able to track her through that."

Dylan reached into his pocket and pulled out his smartphone. "What's her account?"

"I set her up as Niram437," I said.

He thumbed through the app until he found Niram's profile. The screen filled with photos of her posing with students and strangers.

"What's the most recent one?" I asked.

"Hold on, let me check. Weird."

"What?"

"Hard to say. Look for yourself."

I leaned over the smartphone screen. The graffiti image of a phoenix on the side of a building stared back at me. The firebird resembled the lantern design, except this one was a vivid purple. I scrolled through the other photos and they showed Niram posing in front of the graffiti image.

"Where is that?" I asked.

Dylan pointed at the picture. "Look in the background. See the outline of the downtown skyline? I think she's near the river valley."

"The river valley? That's at least a half hour from the school. What's she doing there?"

Dylan shrugged. "No idea."

Grimoire leaned over my shoulder. "Odd that she would recreate her own image."

"And then take selfies with it?" Dylan added.

"I told her to take selfies to get people to notice her. Maybe she's trying to get my attention."

"What does she want to tell you?" Dylan asked.

"I don't know. Scroll through the other photos."

He thumbed through a series of photos of Niram posing with the graffiti art.

"Well, at least now we know her whereabouts," Grimoire said.

"And if she's at the river valley, that means we can get the vacuum," I said.

"She can move swiftly. You had best be careful."

Dylan scratched his head. "Weird."

"What is it?" I asked.

"Now some old woman is posing in front of the graffiti."

Grimoire raised an eyebrow. "Show us."

Dylan flipped the phone around. I stiffened.

"That's my mom," I said. "I have to go. Mr. Grimoire, how do I get out of the vault? I need to see my mom."

"Hold on, Kristina. Calm down. The djinns are shape shifters. They can adopt the guises of the humans they meet."

"What?" Dylan asked.

"They can take the form of the people they see."

"But she's never met Kristina's mom," Dylan said. "Has she?"

"When I set up her Instagram account, I showed her mine. She saw a picture of my mom there."

"At least give your mom a call and see if she's okay," Dylan said.

I fished my phone out of my pocket and dialed.

Mom answered, "Kristina?"

"Mom? Are you all right? Where are you?"

"At home. Waiting for you for the last hour. Kristina, are you okay?" She sounded the same way as she did the day she told me Dad had decided to split. A little fake cheer that barely hid her seething anger underneath.

"Yes, I'm fine."

"Where are you? I can come pick you up."

"No, I'm about to get on the bus," I said. "I'll be home soon."

"We'll talk when you get here," she said.

'Talk' basically meant she was going to yell at me until she was hoarse. I debated whether or not to stay in Grimoire's vault. But I had to be sure my mom was safe. "I'm on my way," I said, then I hung up.

Dylan shook his head. "Is she okay?"

"She is, but I might not be. If I don't show up at school tomorrow, you'll know what happened."

"You'll be putting your mother at risk," Grimoire warned.

"Except Niram may have already found her. I can't leave my mom alone. I have to go."

"Then at the very least take this with you." Grimoire drew a silver-plated business card holder from his inside jacket pocket, clicked it open, and thumbed off a white business card.

I took the card.

Dylan leaned over my shoulder. "Does it turn into a flying carpet or a throwing star?"

"No. Call the number on the card and you'll reach me."

"Oh," Dylan said, losing interest in the card.

"I'll be able to help you if you need me," Grimoire said. "Call if you get any sense of trouble."

"I will."

To say my real mom was upset would be the understatement of the century. She laid into me with a verbal whipping that blistered my ears and turned my face bright red.

"What was so important that you lost track of time?"

"Nothing. Mom, I'm okay. So I wasn't home when you got here. It's no big deal."

"You have no idea what it's like to come home expecting to see someone and they're not there."

"I'm not Dad," I said.

"I couldn't care less about your father," she said.

Then I noticed the object in her hands. Mom

was rubbing the jade carp Lao Lao had given me. I wasn't the only one who needed the charm.

I took her hand. "You miss her, too."

For a few minutes, we just sat together on the couch.

Finally, I broke the silence. "I'm sorry, Mom. Next time, I'll call if I know I'm going to be late."

She patted my hand and gave me back the jade carp.

"No. You keep it for a while," I said.

She smiled and held on to the trinket. "You better go to bed, Kristina. It's been a long day."

I smiled, glad to know she was safe. Niram must have used one of my photos to recreate the image of my mom.

I tossed the cushions off the sofa. Mom helped me pop open the folded mattress inside.

"Kristina, you'd tell me if anything was wrong, right?"

"Yes, Mom. Everything's fine." How could I tell her that I had unleashed a djinn on the world? She'd never believe me.

"Okay. Good night." She walked into her bedroom.

As I climbed into bed, I stared at the Olympic rings of my hair elastics. The green one had fallen onto the nightstand. I picked up the elastic and put it back in its proper place. It seemed like forever ago that I was hanging out with Jen in my old bedroom, making fun of old celebrities with young wives. I missed my room. I missed my friends. I missed my old Niram-free life.

I would trade anything to be back in that house, but I knew that wasn't going to happen. I rolled over and pulled the blanket over my head, but I was too keyed up to fall asleep. Instead, I mulled over the events of the day.

One thing bothered me. If Grimoire's vault was hidden away from everyone's attention, how could Dylan and I break in? Our showing up in the vault seemed too much of a random event. Something didn't add up, and I decided that I had better not turn my back on the keeper of the vault.

The next morning, I got up early and slipped into some clean clothes. I had to find out what Niram was up to, and I didn't want to wait any longer. The streets were busy with commuters driving to their downtown offices. I walked briskly along the sidewalk to my bus stop. My shoes padded across the pavement, creating an odd echo in the morning rush hour.

I stopped and turned. No one was behind me.

I picked up the pace. The phantom footsteps also picked up the pace. I glanced back. Nothing. Eyes seemed to peer out at me from everywhere.

My skin tingled from the sensation of being watched. Had Niram tracked down my apartment? Would she try to attack me in the middle of a busy street? Part of me wanted to rush home, but I didn't want to put Mom in danger.

Instead, I jogged to the bus stop about a half block away, hoping that I'd find some other people already there. Safety in numbers. The phantom footsteps echoed behind me. I slowed when I spotted an old woman in a brown wool overcoat on the bus bench. Perfect.

The lady smiled as I sat next to her. For a second, I thought her eyes were different colours, but she turned away before I could confirm. I didn't want to take any chances so I stood up, searching for an escape route that didn't lead back home.

Then I remembered Grimoire's card. I reached into my back pocket but it wasn't there. I searched the other pocket. Nothing. I began to panic until I realized I wasn't wearing the same pair of pants as yesterday. In my rush to leave, I had left the card behind in my other jeans.

"Something wrong, dear?" the old woman asked.

"I forgot something at home."

"The number 10 is usually late. If you're close, I could sweet talk Larry to waiting a minute or two."

"Thanks, but I should be fine." I glanced up and down the sidewalk for the source of the earlier footsteps. No sign of Niram or anyone else.

"Oh, my!"

I spun around. The old woman's purse had fallen and spilled its contents all over the pavement.

"I'll get that," I offered as she stood up to gather her things.

"Thank you, dear. Oh, oh, oh!" The old woman was shuffling awkwardly toward the street as the oncoming traffic roared past us.

"What are you doing?" I cried, reaching out to stop her.

"Stop! Stop pushing me!" she said, her voice high pitched with terror. There was no one around but me.

I grabbed her arm and pulled her back. A wisp of smoke floated in the air behind her. Suddenly, the woman slid forward until her feet were on the edge of the sidewalk and she teetered toward an oncoming truck. Her eyes met mine.

"Help!" she cried.

I took hold of her arm with both hands and tried to stop her from swaying head first into the path of the truck. The wisp of smoke behind the woman solidified into the inky silhouette of a girl.

Niram.

I angled myself and grabbed the edge of the bench as an anchor, but Niram was too strong. The old woman leaned over the street now. One more push and she'd land in the street. I backpedalled, hoping to out-muscle Niram. No luck. Now the toes of my shoes slid over the edge of the sidewalk.

The truck roared down the right-hand lane. The driver stared down at his lap, probably texting. Our bizarre tug-of-war continued as the smoke silhouette grew bigger and pushed against the woman's back.

I blurted out, "Niram, I wish you'd blow away."

"As you command." Niram's voice echoed in my ears.

The temperature shot up. And waves of heat slammed against me. Then a gust of warm wind roared from the street and blew away the smoke. I pulled the old woman back just as the large truck zoomed past us. We fell to the bench.

"Are you all right?" I asked.

The bewildered woman nodded, barely able to speak. My chest tightened as I scanned the street for any sign of Niram. She had just forced me to use up my second wish.

9: Deal with a Djinn

At school, Dylan waited for me in the parking lot. He paced back and forth in front of the teachers' cars, then rushed over as soon as he saw me jump off the bus.

"What's wrong?"

"Niram made me use my second wish," I said.

He glanced around. "Where is she?"

"I used up a wish to make her blow away."

"What? You wasted your wish on that?"

I explained what happened at the bus stop. Dylan listened intently, gasping when I told him how Niram nearly killed the old woman.

"We have to spirit you to a safe hiding place." He grabbed my arm. His hand felt warm to the touch.

"No, we need the vacuum," I said.

"What?" Dylan let go. "Have you lost your mind? Niram could be anywhere."

"Yes, but we need the vacuum to suck her into the lantern."

He hesitated. "Very well. They haven't unlocked the main doors yet. I believe there is another way in. I need something first. Come with me."

He jogged across the parking lot to the far end of the track, where the scoreboard stood next to a small shed surrounded by shrubs.

"What do you need?" I asked.

"You will see."

As we neared the shed, he slowed down. He moved with a grace I hadn't noticed before. Maybe it was because today he wasn't carrying his longboard. He slipped between some bushes and motioned me to follow.

When we reached the small clearing around the shed, I froze. Graffiti art had been sprayed all over the aluminum siding—with an image of a phoenix much like the one on Niram's Instagram account. The purple firebird spread its wings across the entire shed wall. Under one of its wings was a smaller firebird. Niram had been here.

"Dylan, we have to get out of here."

"Why?" He cocked his head, apparently oblivious to the graffiti.

A horrible thought took hold of me. "Dylan, how did you get to school?"

"I walked."

In the short time I had known him, Dylan had always ridden his longboard to school.

"Are you well, Kristina?" He leaned toward me.

It was then that I noticed the colour of his eyes. One was blue and the other was green.

This wasn't Dylan.

"What's the matter?"

"Nothing. Just...remember what Mr. Grimoire told us yesterday. We should be on the lookout for Niram."

"Don't worry about her," he said.

"No, he said be careful. He said the best way to find her is to close our eyes and sniff for the smoke. Close your eyes, Dylan."

He refused. Instead, he cracked a smile. "You're clever, Kristina. Almost too clever for your own good. When did you determine I wasn't Dylan?

"He always has his longboard."

"Ah. Not that it matters now." Dylan smoothly morphed into the slim form of Niram.

I took a step back, searching for an escape route.

"No need to leave so soon, Kristina. I just want to talk."

"Like you did at the bus stop?"

Niram stopped. "My apologies for that. I acted rashly. I was hoping you might be willing to make a deal."

I took another step back. "Mr. Grimoire told me what you would do once you were free. I believe he used the term 'total destruction.'"

"He hasn't told you the whole story. I just want to enjoy my freedom, that's all. But he took it away from me. Like they all do. They use me for my wishes and then stuff me back into my prison. That's no life for anyone."

"If what you did at the bus stop is a hint of what you'll do when you're free, I can see why Mr. Grimoire put you in the lantern."

"I counted on you to save that old woman," Niram said. "I would have never gone through with pushing her into traffic."

"Yes, I think you would have."

"Such a low opinion of me. How disappointing. Especially when I have a way out for both of us."

"What?"

"Waste your third wish, and I will leave your loved ones alone," Niram offered. "I promise I won't hurt anyone you care about."

"You'll give your word?"

"Djinns must keep their promises. It's a contract."

"That's not what I heard."

"From Grimoire? The fool has it wrong. I'll wager he's told you that we are devious and selective about how we keep our promises."

"Something like that."

Niram sighed. "He's mistaken. Like all the other mortals who have found us. The stories they tell characterize us as evil, but they fail to point to the truth, which is that mortals usually fail to communicate their wishes properly. And this notion that we want to wreak havoc on the world, well Grimoire should be one to talk. You mortals are the ones who will destroy this world."

"You have a low opinion of people. How disappointing," I said, mocking Niram's earlier statement.

"That's because mortals give me every reason to distrust them. The first time I was trapped, I lingered in my prison until I was desperate for companionship. I was so happy when someone set me free, I did everything I could to make them like me."

"You served them."

"Yes, but they didn't see a friend. They saw someone to be used. The first one who set me free was a young widow who had two children and a crushing debt. I helped her out by giving her wealth and riches. When she had more than enough money, she tricked me back into my prison."

"I'm sorry, but not all people are cruel."

"That's what I thought. The next time, a

greedy man with seven sons wanted wives and wealth. I could only give him three wishes, so he forced me back into the lantern and passed it on to his sons. They all used me without a care about the prison I lived in."

"But the stories I've heard about the djinn say that you will wreak havoc on the people who set you free."

"Would you blame me after what I have been through?"

"No, but I wouldn't trust you, either."

"Then it would seem we have come to a crossroads in trust. We can go our separate ways or we can walk down a road together. That is, if you're willing to put aside your prejudices."

"What do you have in mind?" I asked.

"Allow me to make the terms of our agreement so there is no mistaking or misinterpreting."

"Forget it, Niram."

"Trust me, Kristina. This is better than the alternative. I saw the pictures of your friends on your Instagram. I'll find them eventually."

"Don't you dare hurt them," I warned.

"Is that your wish?"

I bit my tongue, refusing to fall for her ploy. "No."

"I'll give you some time to think it over. I'm sure you'll come to the right conclusion."

I ran back to the school. Other students loitered around the schoolyard, waiting for the building to open. Niram sauntered across the field after me. She strolled without a care in the world, but her intense gaze on me suggested she had other things on her mind. The students veered around her. After the run-in with Thorn, everyone was frightened of her. Though she was in the middle of a crowd, she was alone.

Dylan waved at me from just outside the main doors. He held his longboard in one hand and pointed at Niram with the other.

"Do you have a death wish, Kristina?" he asked. "She's here."

"She won't do anything with all the students around. Besides, she wants something from me."

"You talked to her? You *do* have a death wish."

"She wants to trade my last wish for the safety of everyone I know."

He scratched his head. "How?"

I recounted my meeting with Niram. Dylan eyed me with disbelief at first, but he began to nod when I explained her terms. The main doors opened and everyone started to file toward the building. Dylan took me by the arm and led me inside.

"We have to get the vacuum and get to the vault," he said.

He dragged me toward the stairwell, glancing back to see if Niram was coming after us. She strode into the building, her gaze focused not on me, but on Dylan. I pushed him toward the stairs.

"Go," I barked.

We began to climb the stairs. Dylan took two at a time and I tried my best to keep up with him and not trip on the uneven wooden steps. We reached the second floor and I glanced behind me. No sign of Niram. We were safe for now. I wondered why she had let me go.

The fire alarm that began to ring answered my question.

I covered my ears as the alarm ripped through the air. One of the alarms was directly over our heads. "Niram's probably set off the smoke detectors again," I yelled.

"What?"

"I said it must be Niram again!"

"No, it's not. Look!" He pointed down the corridor. Black smoke billowed out of the custodian's office.

10: TORCHED

Dylan dropped his longboard and grabbed a fire extinguisher from the wall while I ran to the custodian's office to see if she was inside. The black smoke filled the hallway and flames licked the doorway. I covered my face with my jacket and inched as close as I could to the searing heat.

"Anyone in there? Hello?"

No answer.

"Mrs. Gavinder! Can you hear me?"

Dylan pushed me aside and fired the extinguisher at the flames. The sizzle of the white foam against the fire sounded like frying bacon. I ducked low and spotted the source of the fire—the vacuum cleaner. There was no sign of Mrs. Gavinder.

The smoke and heat pushed us back down the hallway.

"Did you see anyone in the office?" I asked.

He shook his head. "No, the room's pretty small. We would have seen her."

"Niram set the fire," I said.

"What? How do you know?"

"Because I told her about our plan."

He lowered the fire extinguisher. "Why on earth would you do that?"

"I thought she was you."

"What? Oh. Shape shifter, right," he said. "What do we do now?"

"We have to get to the vault. Maybe Mr. Grimoire knows what to do."

Dylan hoisted the fire extinguisher under his arm and headed toward the stairs. I glanced back at the smoke pouring out of the custodian's office and hoped the vacuum was the only thing Niram was going to burn.

When we got to the stairwell, there was Mrs. Gavinder, huffing and puffing as she ran down the stairs.

"You're alive!" I shouted.

"Yes, yes," she yelled. "But we must go. Out, out, out. Fire."

"We're okay," Dylan explained.

But the custodian wouldn't hear of it. She pushed us toward the stairs and ushered us down.

"Mrs. Gavinder, we have to go up," I said.

"Fire. It's not safe."

There was no arguing with her. We descended as fast as we could. Dylan leaned over and whispered, "Do you think it's her or Niram?"

I glanced over my shoulder at our custodian, trying to get a look at her eyes. Both were brown.

"No, I'm pretty sure it's Mrs. Gavinder," I said, continuing down the stairs.

We joined the students and teachers huddled in different groups outside the building. Fire engine sirens howled from down the street, and two red trucks rolled up to the school parking lot. Firefighters jumped out of the vehicles and uncoiled their water hoses. Students caught the action with their smartphones while teachers tried to herd the kids further back.

Dylan craned his neck trying to spot Niram in the crowd. I scanned the faces of the students around me.

One of the students gasped and pointed at the building. "Look. Another fire's breaking out on the third floor."

Smartphones immediately pointed upward at the smoke pouring out several of the windows near the top floor of the school.

Dylan stiffened. "What if Niram burns down the school? Will it destroy the vault?"

"I'm not sure. That vault seems to exist outside time and space."

"What if you're wrong?"

I hoped for my sake I wasn't.

"We have to get her out of there somehow so we can get into the vault."

I fished my phone out of my pocket. "Wait, I have an idea."

"You're going to call her?" Dylan asked, his eyes wide with disbelief.

"No, but I'm hoping she has her notifications on." I set up for a selfie, then tapped out a message on my phone.

"What are you doing?" Dylan asked.

"Getting Niram's attention, I hope."

He peeked over his shoulder at the message I was typing under the phone: "Willing to talk about last wish but not in school. You come out here."

"You can't give up your last wish, Kristina. It's the only thing protecting us."

"Don't worry. I'm not, but we need to get her out of the building."

More firefighters ran into the building with hoses over their shoulders. I kept a close eye on the doors around the school for Niram. She didn't emerge.

A few minutes later, the black smoke started to turn white. The kids applauded. A half hour later, a couple of firefighters came out of the school. One of them approached our principal.

I checked my smartphone. Sure enough,

Niram had posted a comment under my photo: "Meet me at the shed."

I showed Dylan the message.

"You're not going through with it, are you?"

"Of course not. I'm going into the school while she's waiting for me to show up."

Principal Michaels waved for everyone to settle down. Phones slowly lowered as the students turned their attention to our principal.

"The firefighters were able to put out the fires quickly. The damage has been contained to the second and third floors. It's bad enough for us to shut the school down for the day. We may be able to open the building back up for classes in a few days. If not, we'll find an alternative space. Check the school website for updates. For now, you'll all stay here. Contact your parents or guardians. Let them know what happened. You are to remain in the schoolyard until someone comes to pick you up. No one's to leave the premises until I know they've been in touch with their families. Understood?"

Mutters of agreement from the crowd. People began texting. Dylan nudged me in the ribs. "Over there."

A firefighter who had emerged from the main doors was walking away from the fire engines and the rest of the crew, toward the shed in the field.

"That has to be her. We've got to get up to the vault before Niram figures out the trick."

"I don't think Principal Michaels or the firefighters are going to let us just walk in."

"You know the building better than I do. Is there a way we can get in where no one will notice?"

"There are a couple of options, but the bigger problem is Niram. She won't wait long for you."

"Hopefully we can get to the vault before she figures out the trick."

"Follow me," Dylan said.

He led me away from the school.

"Where are you going?" I asked.

"Setting up a distraction. Let me have your phone." I handed it to him. He snapped a picture of a convenience store across the street. Then he thumbed a message. "Shed is too dangerous for me. Want someplace public. Go here." He sent the message.

"Not bad, Dylan."

"Hey, I'm not just a pretty face." He handed back my phone, picked up the fire extinguisher he had grabbed earlier, and led me toward the other side of the school.

Teachers tried to corral the students. I caught Mr. Carlton's attention to let him know I was around, then I slipped behind Dylan as he pushed through the crowd until it thinned out. He then veered away from the fire engines to the far end of the school, away from the shed. I expected Principal Michaels to yell at us to come back, but there was too much chaos around the parking lot and in the schoolyard. We safely rounded the corner and got away from the crowd.

Dylan found a lower floor window near the far end of the school and took off his jean jacket.

"Hold this against the window as close as you can. Hopefully it will muffle the noise."

"You're going to break into the school?" I asked.

"Let's just say I'm creating air conditioning. Just hold the jacket."

I obeyed, closing my eyes as he swung the extinguisher. The muffled crack of glass filled my ears. Dylan smashed the fire extinguisher into the window again. This time, the glass shattered.

I glanced back at the corner of the school, waiting for a firefighter or a teacher to come around to investigate. I counted my breaths, waiting. One... two... three... four... five... when I reached twenty-five, I relaxed. "No one's coming."

By this point, Dylan had cleared away the jagged glass pieces and laid his jean jacket over the sill.

"Ladies first," he said.

I knelt down, shimmied through the opening and lowered myself onto a counter in the science room. The broken glass crunched under my feet. Dylan handed me the fire extinguisher and jumped in.

"Do we really need this thing?" I asked.

"Not taking any chances with a fire elemental," he said.

He hopped off the counter and helped me down. We tiptoed to the classroom door. The hallway was empty. We crept out and made our way to the stairwell. The main floor was quiet. The snaking hoses ran up the stairs. We followed them to the second level. Above us, the voices of the firefighters echoed down.

"Strangest thing I've ever seen," one of the firefighters said. "In all my years, I've never seen fire behave like this. One minute, the flames are licking up the wall and the next, they retreat and go out by themselves."

"Makes our job easier, though. I'm not complaining."

The firefighters' footsteps grew louder as they came down the stairs. I backed up, pulling Dylan by the back of his T-shirt. We scrambled down the steps to the second floor and hid in one of the nearby classrooms. The firefighters walked past and continued to the main floor.

I glanced out of the window. The crowd was starting to thin out as guardians arrived to pick up the other students. My phone pinged. A message from Niram on my Instagram photo: "I am here. Where are you?"

I showed Dylan the message.

"Good. Now keep her there."

I typed a message: "I'm on my way. Wait there."

No immediate reply.

Dylan pursed his lips. "We should go now." He grabbed my wrist and pulled me to the doorway.

In the hallway, my phone pinged. Niram posted a photo of an apartment building with one message. "New place to meet. Recognize it?"

My home!

The air suddenly felt stale. I tried to catch my breath, but panic seeped into every fibre of my body. Niram was at my apartment. I tried to remember if this was the day Mom had to go to work or if she started late for class.

"It's a trap," Dylan warned. "You go there without the lantern, we're all doomed."

"How bad can it be to give her freedom?" I said. "She promised to leave everyone I know alone."

"If you're wrong, she might go after everyone out of revenge for making her wait. Screw this.

We're going up to the fourth floor now."

Dylan hoisted the fire extinguisher under his arm. We headed out the door and up the stairs to the third floor. It was empty. We rounded the corner and tackled the next flight of stairs. We were almost at the vault.

Suddenly, Grimoire appeared on the landing. He smiled at us as he held up a small pane of glass.

"Well, it certainly took the two of you long enough."

"Niram knows about our plan," I said. "The vacuum cleaner isn't going to work."

Grimoire's expression fell. "That is unfortunate."

"There has to be another way we can trap her," I said.

"What if we put it up against a door window and force her to come after you through the glass?" Dylan suggested.

"Except," Grimoire started to interject.

"No time for exceptions," I said. "She'll be on her way any minute. Give me the glass."

Grimoire started down the steps, but a wall of fire appeared between him and us.

"Ah, mortals. Still think they can outwit the djinn," Niram said, standing behind us. "Now about that final wish."

Dylan stepped in front of me. "You're not going to hurt her."

"Oh, how cute. He's willing to burn for you. Too bad, he's dry as tinder."

"Ow, ow, ow." Dylan squirmed and hopped from one foot to another.

"What's the matter?" I asked.

He began to jump up and down. His runners were smoking.

"Stop that!" I ordered Niram.

"Is that your wish?"

"No," Grimoire yelled. "Dylan, use the fire extinguisher."

Dylan obeyed, coating his shoes with white foam.

"Grimoire, stay out of this," Niram warned. She raised a hand and the wall of fire pushed closer, forcing him back.

"Get out of here," I told Dylan.

He hesitated.

"Now!"

Finally, he began to limp ahead on his tender feet. Niram raised another hand and a ring of fire circled him, forcing him to stay put.

"No one is going anywhere until you use up your last wish, Kristina."

Dylan sprayed the fire extinguisher on the flames, but another wave of flames appeared to replace the ones he put out. Then the fire extinguisher ran out of foam, leaving only the circle of flames.

"I'm out! What do I do now?"

On the stairs, Grimoire retreated from the advancing wall of fire. "Jump through the flames!"

"I can't. It's too hot. Help me!" Dylan cried.

Niram laughed as the smoke detectors went off and the fire alarm blared.

"Stop it," I yelled.

"All you have to do is wish for it," Niram offered.

Grimoire cried out. "The glass. Take it!"

He hurled the pane over the wall of fire. I reached up to catch it. Niram shot her hand up and a column of fire flew out of her fingers, searing the air in front of me. I screeched in pain, shutting my eyes out, but I opened my hands to catch the glass. It brushed against the tips of my fingers and tumbled to the floor. I dove to the ground to save it, but I was too late.

"No!"

The lantern glass, our only hope to imprison Niram, now lay in broken pieces on the floor.

11: THE FINAL WISH

Shards of broken glass littered the floor. The prison that was supposed to hold Niram was now nothing but debris. I climbed to my feet. The flames seared all around us and the fire alarm blared. Dylan whimpered as the flames closed in. Grimoire had been pushed back to the landing.

"Let them go," I ordered.

"Is that your final wish?" she asked.

Grimoire shouted, "No! She'll wreak destruction on the world. She's a monster."

"Liar," Niram shot back. "My kind has only ever wanted to be free. You mortals are the monsters. Using us and then stuffing us into prisons."

"Kristina, if you set her free, no one will be safe."

Dylan howled. I couldn't let him die.

Grimoire shouted, "Kristina, get Dylan to jump through the flames and come up here. I can pull him to safety in the vault."

Niram screamed, "Enough from you, Grimoire." She shot her hand forward and the wall of flames advanced on Grimoire so quickly that he had no choice but to fall back into the safety of the vault.

"No!" Niram cried out. "I will have my revenge for what you have done to my kind. You will live with the scorch marks of guilt for allowing your wards to die."

She turned toward me and raised her hands.

"Duck!" yelled Dylan.

Instinctively, I dropped to my knees as the fire extinguisher sailed over my head and slammed into Niram's gut. She lost her concentration and the flames died out.

"Up the stairs, Dylan!" I yelled as I rushed to tackle Niram.

He scrambled to the stairs, hesitating when he saw the flames on the landing.

"The fire," he called back. "It's too hot."

"Then get out of the school!"

Dylan ran down the stairs, two at a time while I tried to wrestle the stunned Niram to the floor. She recovered, her blue eye flaring as she growled. A stiff blow to my sternum drove the air out of my chest. I gasped as I doubled over.

"You can't save him," Niram said, panting. "Not unless you wish it."

I crawled across the floor, still gasping for air. The broken glass cut into the palms of my hands. I bit down on my lip to keep from screaming, and I kept moving. The glass shards dug into my palm like tiny little needles. A couple of feet away, a chunk of the pane remained intact. I inched forward.

"There is no escape, Kristina." Niram took a step toward me.

I rolled over on my back to face her, edging myself backward hoping to cover the chunk of glass with my hand.

"There is, as long as I buy him time to get away."

Finally, my hand touched the glass and I pulled it close to my thigh, wedging it out of sight.

"You want to save your friend? You know what to do." She laughed as she turned into a column of smoke and flowed down the stairs after Dylan.

I pocketed the chunk of glass as I climbed to my feet and staggered down the stairs. Firefighters rushed past me with the hoses, responding to the blaring alarm. I pointed up the stairs. "The fire sparked up there."

"You okay, kid?" one of the firefighters asked.

"I'm fine," I said, waving her off.

The firefighters headed up while I made the rest of the way down to the main floor. I stepped over the hoses and headed to the front doors, frantically looking around for Dylan. No sign of him anywhere.

Outside the school, the fire engine was parked back near the building. The schoolyard was empty. I hoped Dylan had gotten away. I wondered where Niram had gone. The answer came when my phone pinged.

Niram had sent a selfie of herself, posing next to the shed. Crumpled on the ground under the graffiti was Dylan. His form was lined up right under the smaller phoenix under the wing of the purple firebird.

Panic took hold and I wanted to sprint over to the shed, but something about the picture calmed me. The way Dylan looked curled up in a ball almost reminded me of a baby in a fetal position, but what caught my eye was how the smaller phoenix looked up at the purple firebird. It was like a chick with its mouth open waiting for its mother to feed him. No, it was the look a child gives a parent.

The truth seeped into my limbs and gave them a new strength. I had been looking at the images the wrong way. They were messages but not for me.

An idea formed. I wasn't sure it was going to work, but this was no time to second guess. I clicked off the app and a fresh stab of pain radiated from my palm. Slivers of glass had imbedded into my flesh. I ignored them as I fished the chunk of glass from my pocket.

Carefully, I inserted the glass between the edge of my smartphone and the rubber cover, so that the chunk was flush against the screen. The glass slipped a few times between my fingers, but I finally managed to lodge it into the phone cover. The glass dangled at an angle against the screen, but it was flush. It was a part of the phone—at least, that's what I tried to convince myself.

Now to test my idea. I stumbled across the field to the bushes. Pushing my way through the foliage, I steeled myself for the final wish. In the distance, the fire alarm blared, but I shut out the noise, focusing my attention on what was before me.

Niram stood over the prone form of Dylan. He began to stir, coughing from smoke that was rising up around his body.

She smiled at me. "I see you got my message."

"Yes. Let Dylan go."

"Is that your final wish?"

"No."

She shook her head as she raised her hands.

Tendrils of smoke rose around my friend, growing in number and coiling around his body. He coughed, trying to expel the smoke from his lungs, but it was too thick. Dylan rose to his knees, but the cloud rose to his head, choking him.

"I'm told the worst way to die is to be burned alive," Niram claimed. "The second is to suffocate. I'm not particular about which way your friend goes. I'll leave that choice up to you."

"Let him go."

She beamed.

"Your wish is my command."

"I'm not wishing for it. I'm asking you."

Her smile faded, replaced with an expression of confusion. "You don't care about your friend? Perhaps, this will change your mind." She snapped her fingers and the cloud of smoke around Dylan thickened. He stood up and waved his hands frantically to clear away the smoke but he was losing the battle.

"Dylan!" I called out.

"Can't...breathe...help!" he gasped, keeling over.

"Make your final wish," Niram said as she casually twirled her finger. "I'll make it simple for you. Save Dylan and set me free."

"Clear out the smoke."

She smiled. "Is that your final wish?"

Dylan's body now writhed on the ground, his hands clawing at his neck for air.

"You don't have the luxury of time, Kristina," Niram said.

"I wish you could have my final wish."

"What?" Niram asked.

"I want you to have my last wish. It's my gift to you."

"Is that your final wish, Kristina?"

I nodded. "Yes. Just do me a favour and clear the smoke."

"As you command."

She beamed as she waved her hand. "No one has ever given me a wish. I don't even know where to begin. This is incredible."

"What about Dylan?"

"Oh right. Him." She waved her hand dismissively.

The smoke blew away, leaving Dylan wheezing and sucking in air. His breathing rattled like an old car engine breaking down. I rushed over and rubbed his back, helping him recover.

"Take it easy, Dylan. You're going to be all right."

"You wasted your last wish," Dylan wheezed.

"Nothing gets past Captain Obvious," I said, trying to lighten the mood.

Niram clapped her hands. "Free at last. And

now to take care of the people who caused me the most grief." She advanced on us.

"But you have your freedom and a wish," I said.

"Now I need your help to get Grimoire. His vault protects him from my magic. I hope he cares as much for your well-being as you did for your friend." She advanced on us.

"Wait, wait," I pleaded. "I know why you posted the pictures."

"They were for you."

"Not the ones of the firebird. You're reaching out. Trying to find out if there are others like you."

She paused.

"I know what it's like. I used to post photos all the time to reach out to my friends from my old school. Jen, Gloria, Rachel. When I came to this school, I was alone just like you were when you showed up. I felt lonely because no one here knew me or cared about me. When I posted my photos, it was like I was reaching out to my old life. And when someone liked the photo, I didn't feel alone anymore. I knew there was someone out there who saw me and cared. You're sending out the photos to see if there are other djinns."

"There are no others. I'm the last of my kind."

"No. Your dad is still here. Trapped in the vault. I saw him. Purple head. Scars across the top. A hook nose."

"I never want to see him again. When I needed him most, he abandoned me."

Her words echoed in my ears with aching familiarity. I had said the same words many times after my dad had left.

"But he's trapped like you," I said.

"He had a chance to save me from Grimoire's trap, but instead he fled. Used the distraction to try to flee. He discarded me."

"Don't you want to tell him how you feel, Niram? Don't you want to know why? You can find out. Grimoire has him in a lamp."

"You're like all the other mortals. Trying to trick me."

I shook my head. "I know what it's like to have your life taken away."

"He is nothing to me."

"I don't believe you," I said. "Otherwise, you wouldn't be drawing the graffiti."

She eyed her artwork on the shed wall.

"That's you. Under your father's wing, isn't it?"

She said nothing.

"Even though he abandoned you, he's still your dad."

Her eyes welled with tears and they sizzled and steamed as they dripped down her cheeks.

"I'm alone," she croaked. "In a world that is not my home."

"I know how you feel. My mom made me move into this neighbourhood. I'm at a new school where no one knows who I am or cares who I am. And all I want to do is get back to my old home and old friends, but that's not possible, because my mom made me move here. But when I reached out, I found a new friend."

Dylan managed a smile and a wave. "Hey, there."

"Niram, maybe you just need to look at what is in front of you."

She narrowed her gaze. "You? Trickery, this is."

"I have no wishes left and no reason to want to befriend you. I could have taken Dylan and run. Instead, I'm still here."

"You..." Her eyes shifted left and right as she tried to sort out my motivation. "I..."

"You keep sending photos of your graffiti out there, but if you want people to notice, put yourself in the pictures. I'll help. We can take a selfie together."

"Why?"

"Because we're going to be friends. And if I

can, I'll help you find out if there are other djinns out there. There have to be. You can't be the last of your kind."

"Grimoire said I was the last."

"What if he was lying?"

She considered this, her eyebrows furrowing.

"Come on, Niram. The more pictures of you we post, the greater the chances of reaching out to one of your own."

She nodded. "I would like that."

I pulled out the smartphone and carefully pressed my fingers against the glass to keep it from falling out. Then I stood beside Niram and put my arm around her shoulder as I lifted the phone to take our picture. "Don't you wish you could be in there forever?"

"In where?"

"In the phone. On the Internet. You can reach out to the entire world with the push of one button. You could find one of your own kind without the fear of being trapped by the humans you talk to."

"I'd like that very much."

I repositioned the phone. "Then let's make it so now. We'll take a selfie and put it out on the web for everyone to see. This might be the one that reaches another djinn."

She smiled and allowed me to stand beside

her with the phone. I held it high over our heads to snap the picture, hoping the glass chunk stayed in place.

"The phone gives you all you want without any of the problems of dealing with mortals."

The chunk began to slide out of the cover. I shifted my thumb to keep it in place. Niram raised an eyebrow at me.

"What are you waiting for? Take the selfie."

Finally, the glass chunk slid back into place. I had to hold it with my thumb.

"Right. Just making sure I have the right angle. Wouldn't you want to be inside the phone, Niram? That would be the ultimate."

"Yes," she said wistfully. "I wish I could be in there."

"Your wish is your command," I said—and snapped the photo.

"What?" Niram's eyes widened at the sight of the chunk. "You tricked me!"

Her skin ignited into flames as she transformed into the firebird. I backed away, getting some distance between Dylan and myself.

"I will burn you to a crisp!" she roared.

I couldn't let go of the phone without the glass chunk falling off. This was the only piece that made the phone a prison for Niram. I pressed my thumb against the glass so it jammed into the cover and held my phone high over my head. I closed my eyes against the blistering heat. My hand felt like it was going to melt off, but I refused to let go.

The air singed. I screamed in pain as my hand burned. Then there was nothing. No sound. I opened my eyes. The bushes were black. Dylan's body smoked, but he was alive. In my hand, the smartphone had survived the blast of heat.

"Kristina!" Dylan yelled. He climbed to his feet and staggered toward me, his clothes singed and his face covered in soot. Otherwise, he was okay.

He hugged me.

"Ugh, you smell like a campfire," I said.

Dylan pulled away. "Sorry. Hey, where is Niram?"

"Right here," I said. I held up the smartphone. The screen was dark and nothing worked, but the device still felt warm in my hand and the chunk of glass was still attached to the cover.

Back at the vault, I explained everything to Grimoire. When he heard about my last-ditch effort to trick Niram, he applauded.

"Well done, Kristina. Well done." He held out

his hand. "I'll take that if you don't mind. I think it would be best if I held it here for safekeeping. Don't you agree?"

"You owe me a new smartphone," I said.

"I'm sure we can come to some kind of arrangement." He began to turn.

"Wait. Where are you going to put her?" I asked.

"Most likely in a case similar to the one that holds her father."

I eyed the display case that held Lapulis Azure. "You know instead of replacing my phone, I'd call things even if you did me one favour."

"Which is?"

"Why bother creating a new case when you can just put her in the one with her father?"

"Two djinns together? That would be dangerous."

I shook my head. "Niram was trying to get out because she wanted to reach out to others like her. If you put her in with Lapulis Azure, she'll have no reason to want to get out."

"An intriguing theory, Kristina. Take away her reason to come out and take away the danger."

Dylan puffed up his chest. "Hold on just a minute. This djinn tried to make barbecue out of us and you want to help her? Why?"

I eyed Lapulis Azure's lamp. "I guess I feel

like someone owes her something." If I couldn't get answers from my dad, I hoped Niram might get some closure from hers.

Grimoire smiled and walked to the display case with the lamp and unlocked the case. He placed the phone right beside the lamp.

"Thank you, sir," I said.

He gave me a knowing nod. "You are an exceptional caretaker, Kristina."

I took one last look at the phone. I hoped Niram would be able to make peace with her father. At least, she had the chance I never did.

"You did well, both of you. Now to get you back."

"Will we be able to visit the vault again, Mr. Grimoire?" I asked.

"It's your obligation now."

I cocked my head, confused.

"All explanations will come in due time," he said.

I wasn't sure if the room was still a little too warm from the trapped elementals, but I did know that his cryptic smile made my palms suddenly sweat.

Epilogue

Students whispered that the ghosts had started the fire in the school, but the investigators concluded that faulty wires and not paranormal arsonists were the cause of the blaze.

The top of the school was off limits while the crews repaired the fire damage, which meant that Dylan and I couldn't get up to the vault for a couple of weeks. I used the downtime to recover and to play some classic video games with Dylan. At home, I rearranged my nightstand so that I could add one more souvenir to the rings on the jewellery tree. It was Dylan's hemp bracelet.

Three weeks later, the building reopened and we could move from our temporary classrooms to our school. The first thing I wanted to do was see Grimoire. Dylan and I headed up to the fourth floor and squeezed through the gap and into the weightless void.

When I emerged in the vault, something was wrong. No one was here and it looked like the place had been ransacked. I walked over the broken statues and stepped around a pile of junk. Dylan surveyed the damage.

"Do you think Niram broke out?" he asked.

"I don't know."

"Where is Mr. Grimoire?"

"Mr. Grimoire," I called out. No answer.

Dylan and I searched the vault for the tall man. So many of the artefact cases were broken. Some items were gone while others were tossed carelessly on the floor. I picked up what I could and reset the items in their cases. In the far corner, a body was slumped on the floor. I rushed over, waving at Dylan to join me. The tweed jacket gave away the owner. It was Grimoire. I knelt over him and gently rocked him back and forth.

"Ow," he groaned.

"Are you okay, sir? What happened here?"

"Kristina? Dylan?"

"What happened here?" Dylan asked as he helped Grimoire to his feet.

"Betrayal. Someone I thought I trusted has turned her back on me. It explains much but raises questions about even more."

"I don't understand, sir," I said.

"Did Niram escape?" Dylan asked.

"I'm afraid it is much worse than that. There was an intruder."

"Who?"

"I'm sorry to pull you both into this. I had hoped it wouldn't have to come to this."

"What, sir? Are we in danger?"

He paused and looked into my eyes. "I'm afraid you might be."

Dylan glanced around the room. "How? From who?"

Grimoire motioned us to take him to one of the overturned divans. Dylan and I set it back on its legs then helped him into the red seat. He sat down and rubbed the back of his neck.

"Kristina, I had planned on retiring from looking after the vault," he said. "I was looking for a replacement. Someone who had the skills and fortitude to manage the collection. I thought I had found the right person. She was my apprentice and I had expected that she was almost ready to take over, but we argued over whether or not the vault pieces should remain hidden from the world. She had the idea that she could sell a few pieces and I disagreed."

"Why would anyone want to sell these things?" I asked. "They're dangerous."

"You are astute, Kristina. That was my argument, but Rebecca saw things differently. We had a falling out and she left my employ a few days before you and Dylan happened upon my vault. I believe she was the one who did all of this."

"Why?" Dylan asked.

"I suspect she has taken away some of the prized artefacts for her own. I believe she intends to put them on the black market to sell to the highest bidder. Under no circumstances can I allow this to happen. They are far too dangerous to be in the hands of mere mortals. I'm going to have to retrieve them, and I'm going to need help."

"I will do what I can," I said.

"Me, too," Dylan added.

"The problem is I'm not sure if the two of you are...right for the job."

"I just risked my life to get your djinn back in the prison!"

He nodded. "True, but I believe it was no accident that you gained access to the vault. I believe my apprentice let you in. Your presence distracted me from what she was doing."

"I didn't know anything about the vault until I got here. You think I'm working with your old assistant?"

"No, but I think you are a pawn Rebecca will try to exploit again."

"Now that I know about her, I won't let her use me. Sir, I want to help."

"Then you had better prepare yourself, because this will be quite the ordeal." He stood up and picked up a broom. "The first thing we are going to have to do is clean up and find out exactly what she has taken."

"How are we going to find Rebecca?" Dylan asked.

Grimoire examined the items on the floor and walked to an empty display case. He turned pale. His hand rested on the broken glass. "With what she has stolen, I believe we will know soon enough."

To be continued ...

Deklin